WOODSTOK FARLEY

The Water Stop Saloon
More Wandering Tales

Copyright © 2022 by Woodstok Farley

All rights reserved. No part of this publication may be reproduced, stored or transmitted in any form or by any means, electronic, mechanical, photocopying, recording, scanning, or otherwise without written permission from the publisher. It is illegal to copy this book, post it to a website, or distribute it by any other means without permission.

First edition

This book was professionally typeset on Reedsy. Find out more at reedsy.com

*For Laurie Jo Green and Elaine Platt -
My two beautiful sisters who are gone, but I will never forget.*

Contents

Picasso Hangin' at the Water Stop Saloon	1
Paid in Full	13
Go West, Young Longhair, Go West	35
Burying a Cat in an Oklahoma Winter	49
Closet Plants	61
Haulin' Glass	77
The Glass Factory Menagerie	95
The Case of the Murder of the Salesman	115
The Case of the Bad Country People	129
Peeing on the Chairman of the Board's Shoes	145
I'll Remember You No More	155
Quarantined	167
The Cowboy and the Hippy Chick	189
Acknowledgments	201
About the Author	203

I

Picasso Hangin' at the Water Stop Saloon

A Romanian museum is analyzing ashes found in a stove to see if they are the remains of seven paintings by Picasso, Matisse, Monet, and others that were stolen last year from the Netherlands...It was the biggest art theft in more than a decade [with] an estimated value of tens of millions of dollars...[Among the] stolen paintings were: Picasso's 1971 Harlequin Head...(AP July 2013).

Freight Car Bob has been hoboin' since he ran away from home as a young boy. Hopping trains to points unknown was always the excitement he initially craved. "Ya' never knowed where ya'd end up at," he would always say to anyone who asked why he hoboed. "And endin' up where you ain't never been 'afore is just 'bout as excitin' as findin' a brand new penny. It don't get no better even ifn' ya' got a pocket full." Freight Car always found himself persuasive with others, persuasive that is when it came to trading or bartering for whiskey. With any item in tow, he would march right in, slap the item on the bar and strike a deal with a grin that said: "let's bargain."

Like the time he traded a wheelchair for a whole bottle of Johnny Walker. Freight Car said he found it after one of those tent revival-healing meetings held on the outskirts of town. He said the owner no longer needed it. Freight Car convinced the bartender that it would make great entertainment, and he was right. Everyone who came in wanted to take a spin around the bar or just like the idea of staying stationary and raising the front wheels off the floor in an attempt to balance on the large back wheels. The more beer you drank, the harder it got. Why, they even hold an annual Wheelchair Olympics in the bar. The locals devised a series of competitions, mostly involving some sort of obstacle course in and around the tables, often ending at the jukebox. Freight Car was made the honorary Olympic torchbearer. Whenever he found himself in town, the locals would push him around the bar in that wheelchair with a Bic lighter held high in his hand and celebrated him with free whiskey.

Outside of Monahans, Texas, there was a local watering hole—the Water Stop Saloon. It was built after the tracks were completed in 1928. Without much forethought, they built the saloon right up close to the tracks so that when a train rolled by, the bottles on the shelves would all rattle. Now since there was a well-kept schedule for the trains and the fact that the saloon had no clock, the patrons would all holler out the time when the rattling began, "9:17!" or "12:05!" When the 2:11 ran, the bartender gave the last call.

Kelsey McClemmons had owned the Water Stop Saloon since 1972 when he bought it from the retiring owner. That previous owner was the one who used the train schedule instead of clocks. He had been a railroad man himself and liked the idea of everyone shouting out the schedule. Kelsey kept it that way. He said, "I got me a bunch of cuckoos' and usin' them as clocks just makes sense."

The saloon patrons at the Water Stop are an interesting mix of folks. There are the workers getting off a 10-hour shift and not ready for going home yet. There are the single men who brag about taking someone home for the night, but mostly it ends up just brag. And there are the lonely, unattached women who hope beyond hope for a decent man to fill more than one night, but mostly their morning's end up eating breakfast alone—braggarts aren't interested in relationships. Sometimes a few couples come for the cheap entertainment. Whiskey's cheap, dancing's free, and the Motel 6 has a continental breakfast for no additional charge. Finally, there are the occasional drunks who are just looking for the liquid numbness to silence whatever pain or lost love drove them to drink in the first place. Freight Car, well…he just likes to drink.

One afternoon before the usual lunch crowd, Kelsey saw Freight Car come in, struggling with what appeared to be a large painting. It took Freight Car a few minutes to figure out how to navigate the door, but he finally managed it and looked up at Kelsey. The frame holding the painting looked to be very ornate and gilded—perhaps with gold. The painting itself looked like one of those abstract portraits of a man's head. The head had a sort of a green floppy hat, and his eyes were too close together, almost cross-eyed and not aligned. He also had a high white collar covering a long skinny neck. In fact, the whole face appeared to be skinny and in need of a shave. Kelsey's first thought was that the artist wasn't very talented. He also wondered what Freight Car was doing with this painting. Maybe he painted it. Then he saw the *let's bargain* grin. Freight Car said he found the painting in the scrub brush not far from the train tracks. He had heard about a derailment a few months back and figured there might be something worth trading hiding in the brush. He was right.

"Now Kelsey, this 'yer paintin' is worth more than this 'yer whole saloon," he exclaimed, waving his arm across the room. "Why anyone can tell this frame is solid gold," while banging his knuckles on a non-metal-sounding frame.

Realizing that to get into an argument with Freight Car while he was in bargaining mode was an exercise in futility, Kelsey quickly gave in.

"Freight Car, that frame ain't no solid gold. In fact, it probably is nothin' more than spray paint. But seins' how it's you, I'll spot you a beer. After all, you went through all the trouble to haul it in here through the front door. Not sure where to hang it, though. Maybe the men's john?"

Freight Car frowned at the thought of his treasure being relegated to the men's bathroom. The idea of this abstract man looking down at him while he was using the facilities creeped him out, even if it was a painting. He then began to survey the walls of the saloon for the appropriate place to display his latest treasure. He decided it would be most appropriate hanging next to the dartboard, in place of the poster advertising *Beer Made From Pure Rocky Mountain Spring Water*. This was west Texas, and no one drank anything but Lone Star beer, he reasoned.

"Well, it's a damn sight worth more than one beer. Hell, feel the weight of it. Come on now, surely you can do better than a beer? How about a bottle of yur' cheap-ass whiskey? Come on now, be a sport. You know'd I always brings you my best stuff."

Then Freight Car hefted the painting up next to the dartboard and turned to see if Kelsey admired the place he had picked to display this work of art. Kelsey just shook his head and reached under the bar for a half-full bottle of bar whiskey.

"I'll trade you this and no more," holding the bottle up and swinging it from side to side by its neck to entice Freight Car. The bargain was struck, although Freight Car grumbled that "it weren't fair."

Leaning the painting against the wall below the dartboard

and taking the bottle, Freight Car headed to a quiet corner near the back of the saloon, still muttering under his breath, that Kelsey got the best of him.

About that time, the mill-working lunch crowd came in the door full of conversation and greetings to Kelsey. They invited Freight Car over to join them and to hear about his wanderings. Freight Car quickly pointed out his latest acquisition leaning against the wall looking for some complimentary voices to bolster his displeasure of only receiving half a bottle of whiskey for all his efforts. Most of the workers remembered the train derailment, and they also agreed with Freight Car that the painting was quite a find. Jim Ed, in fact, remembered more than most, since he worked as a volunteer firefighter and was on the scene that day.

"Yeah, I was there and heard that some of the cargo that got spilt was valuable art. I'm bettin' that this here is one of 'em," he said, pointing with his beer at the abstract painting.

Freight Car gave Kelsey a smug look as he tipped his glass slowly to his lips to emphasize the fact that his find was worth much more. Kelsey ignored him but decided if he didn't want to hear Freight Car's going on and on, he better hang the damn painting. Grabbing a hammer he kept under the bar, Kelsey hung the painting right next to the dartboard, hoping that would please Freight Car and hold off more of his grumbling. Freight Car leaned back in his chair to admire the painting and then smiled as he raised his glass to Kelsey with approval.

Later as the night crowd started spilling in, Harold and Judy were dancing slowly to "Folsom Prison Blues." It was the previous owner that had the jukebox loaded with train songs.

Judy whispered in Harold's ear, "Sweetheart, can't you dance a little faster!"

Now Judy knew she was fortunate that Harold even danced at all. He normally preferred to sit in some dark out-of-the-way corner unnoticed since he and Judy were both married—but not to each other. Slow song, fast song, it didn't matter. Harold had one speed. They had started coming to the Water Stop a couple of months ago while Judy's husband was on one of his frequent out-of-town trips and Harold's wife was at St. Francis bingo night.

"Now Judy, you know there ain't no need to draw attention to ourselves."

"Harold, everyone here knows us, and they all know we are not married to each other. The only ones who don't know about us are our spouses. Even the clerk at the Motel 6 knows our names are not Mr. and Mrs. George Bush. In fact, I think it's time we tell Gail and Ben. I don't want to meet only on bingo night. I want to go have breakfast together even if it's only a continental one and not sneak out in the middle of the night to our own beds."

Harold agreed with Judy, but he knew the divorce would be nasty, and he simply didn't want to go through that in such a small town. Besides, Gail's daddy owned a lot of oil wells and Gail, after all, was an only child. He stood to lose a fortune if he divorced.

Grady Benson was a drunk. He started drinking after inheriting a small fortune from an aunt who always thought he would go somewhere if only he had the money. Grady never went anywhere except to the Water Stop to, as he put it, "drink to keep in shape." After all, Grady considered himself a professional drinker. He said, "if there was an Olympic event for drinking,

I'd win me a gold every time."

Grady and Harold had grown up together in the same town. They had been rivals all their lives. They were rivals in 4-H. They were rivals in Rodeo Club. They were rivals on the field, and they were rivals for the affection of Judy. In high school, Judy had dated Grady, but she went to prom with Harold. Everyone thought they would marry right after college, but Judy married Ben, an Oklahoma State senior, after a bottle of tequila introduced them on a Spring Break in Mexico. Harold never got over it. Grady never got over Harold taking Judy to prom. And now, here they were dancing at the Water Stop. It really got Grady's goat. He was determined to have at least one dance with the lady he lost.

"Pardon me, ma'am. Reckon I could have me just one dance?" Grady said, bowing slightly to Judy.

"Get lost, Grady. I'm with Judy, and she ain't dancin' with nobody but me. 'Specially not with no drunk."

"I was addressin' the lady, not you."

"Well, I said she ain't dancin', and that's final. Now hit the road!"

"How 'bout we throw for it?"

"I ain't throwin' no darts with you, Grady. Now just get and leave us the hell alone."

Judy had had enough and left Harold and Grady arguing on the dance floor. Harold knew that the evening would not end at Motel 6.

While Harold and Grady were arguing, Reverend Connolly, of the local Episcopal parish, came in for his evening nightcap. The Reverend had been coming in for his nightcap since his wife left the church for the tongue-talking, snake handling, dancing in the aisle Pentecostal Holiness Church of Last Days. She had volunteered to be the keeper of the snakes between services, and the Reverend just couldn't face all that rattling in his bedroom at night. His wife said the snakes were calmer in the dark, quiet room than with all the lights and television noise in the den. The bedroom was quieter also because they quit having sex. The Reverend said the sex was no longer genuine. He said he could no longer distinguish between ecstasy and Charis-mania—as he likes to call it. He always believed both were fake.

"Evening, Harold. Evening Grady. What are you both fussing about this time?"

"Evenin' Reverend. We's just havin' us a little discussion 'bout dancin' and throwin' darts. 'Cain't seem to come to the same conclusion 'cause Harold here don't want a throw 'gainst me," Grady offered.

"I ain't throwin' against no ass—," Harold stopped as he realized who he was addressing, "against no jerk who just wants to show off his throwin' skills."

Leaning in to whisper to Harold, the Reverend offered, "It might be a way to get Grady to end the discussion. Besides, everyone knows his aim is off when he's downed a few. What do you say?"

It was decided, and the two stood behind the line Kelsey had painted on the wood floor because of official rules. Everyone took notice and moved out of the line of fire, that is, everyone but Jim Ed, who was at the bar ordering his usual last drink of Jameson's neat before going home. He turned from the bar and walked into the line of throwing just as Harold let fly his first dart. Jim Ed howled as the dart struck him in his arm just above the elbow, spilling his whiskey.

"Damn you, Harold! You owe me another whiskey," he yelled as he pulled the dart out and threw it back at Harold, barely missing him. "Probably gonna have to get me a Tetanus shot now!" Jim Ed turned back to the bar and ordered another whiskey and loudly proclaimed that it was on Harold's tab.

"Sorry about that, Jim Ed," then turning to Grady, he said, "That one don't count. I get another."

"The hell you do. You took your shot. It don't matter none ifn' your target was movin' or not. It's my turn."

Now everyone knew that Grady was the best at throwing darts. He was the champion of the whole county. He never missed, that is, as long as he was sober. But he wasn't sober. Squinting at the dartboard and practicing his throw without releasing, Grady knew he'd had one too many. But his reputation was on the line, and besides, he had made such an ass of himself in front of Judy. He released a practice throw which went wide and stuck in the right eye of Freight Car's painting.

"Well, seein' how each of us missed the board guess one more throw stands to reason. Whoever makes this throw gets the last dance with the lady," declared Grady.

Confident of Grady's drunk, Harold muttered, "Throw."

Now, as mentioned, Grady is a good throw when he is sober. He often made impossible shots that few had ever if ever, made. Why, once in a throw against some fella from Ireland, Grady made the near-impossible shot of throwing one dart into the flight of his previous throw. This time he made the conscious effort of keeping his grip on the barrel until he was ready to release. By now, the whole bar had gathered around to watch the competition. Many were betting on Grady. Sober or drunk, Grady knew darts.

Grady closed his left eye, and, saying a prayer under his breath, he let the dart fly. It flew straight, straight into the flight of his previous throw. Two yellow darts now hung from the right eye of the painting. Grady hung his head in shame even though it was truly a beautiful shot if he had planned it.

Harold smiled as his throw landed him on the board this time, and he raised his arms in a victory motion as he turned to see if Judy had witnessed the triumph. She was nowhere to be seen.

Several days later, Judy's father, who considered himself a bigshot, walked into the Water Stop and noticed the painting with two darts sticking out of the canvas. He walked over and slowly examined the painting leaning in from time to time to admire the brush strokes. Standing back, he commented to Kelsey, "Bet it was Grady what made that shot in this here Picasso." Freight Car was sitting in the corner. He raised his eyebrows and looked at Kelsey, then at the empty bottle in front of him.

II

Paid in Full

It was dark on Lake Keystone in northeastern Oklahoma. Clouds had moved in and blocked what little light the stars might offer on a moonless night. The wind was blowing just enough to raise the wake from its rest. An occasional lone duck bobbed with the rhythm, rocking slightly to the right and then to the left. If you listened carefully, you could hear the hypnotic waves lapping the rocky shoreline, and if you listened even deeper into the unconscious night sounds, you could barely hear the sputtering of a Honda 45 HP motor pushing the light blue and white '67 Larson Runabout out into deeper water away from the shallow lagoon and the docks. Two figures stood at the helm, but unlike the ducks, one awkwardly adjusted his stance with the rhythm of the lake, and the other showed more grace on the water, perhaps from experience. If you were close enough, you could see the distinction between the two. One was bigger in build—think offensive lineman bigger, but maybe middle-aged—with a receding hairline that many men his age seem to experience. His manner of dress was casual, like someone who purposefully shopped at a chain department store not for the prices so much as for blending with the masses. In other words, if this man passed you in a crowd, you would never notice anything definite about him except maybe his size.

Now the other guy, the one piloting the boat, the one more comfortable with the boat's rhythm, had an air of a man who dressed for show. His opened large red and white flower Hawaiian shirt blew between his arms like a cape. This was a man who, even though the style may have passed, kept his clothing because, as he liked to say, "I spent good money, so why throw it away just because it's gone out of style?" He wore his hair long because of some long-ago rebellion, although he would quickly add:

"You seen the price of a haircut nowadays? It's downright criminal what they charge for a damn haircut that grows back in a few weeks, and then you got to spend the money all over again! Hell, I can put my money to better use. Money don't come easy. Shit, everybody knows that."

Take the old Larson Runabout he was piloting. When brand new, it was the finest boat for the money. Even though the blue paint on the hull had faded over the years, and the white bow stripe had lost its sheen from exposure to the sun, it still took him anywhere on the lake he wanted to go.

"Yes, sir. Best money I ever spent. Just a little TLC, and she fires up every time."

But tonight, the motor appeared to be agreeing with its age, or was it way past its prime even though care had been given to it for years, long after the mechanic said it would last. Yeah, tonight, it too, might die.

Accompanying the men in the boat was a metal barrel. You know, the fifty-five-gallon type, painted a bright blue complete with white and red hazard stickers warning of previous contents. The barrel sat firmly on the deck as if the contents were heavy enough to keep it stable. Every once in a while, the balding man would look back over his shoulder at the barrel, perhaps to make sure the contents didn't spill out. He seemed preoccupied with the barrel as if it were not his choice to bring it along.

"You sure this is how you want to do this?" the big man asked over the sound of the sputtering engine.

"Would you relax? I told you I wanted him drowned. I want him to die miserably, after all the money and aggravation he cost me, and drowning him in a barrel at the bottom of the lake is what I want. No, he's got to be killed slowly. This is how I want it. Now I paid you good money for this, so no arguments," said the boat driver. However, his last comment didn't seem quite so assured of his position in this scheme. Here he was telling a professional hitman what to do. Who's to say the hitman wouldn't do the same to him? After all, even though he had paid the man upfront, the hitman did object when the plan was first laid out to him. Thinking back a few hours earlier, when they stood in the newly constructed add-on room, he remembered their conversation.

"That's not an efficient way to kill a man. Lots can go wrong. I been in this business long enough to know that some things may sound good, but they just don't work out the way you plan. What if the barrel decides one day to float to the surface? Water will hold its secrets until it doesn't. Did ya think of that? I have. I got a reputation to keep. In my business, I can't afford no screwups. We don't need that kind of heat."

"All we gotta do is put some holes in the barrel, and problem solved," the other man said as he gestured with the raising of his hands spread shoulder-width and shrugging the right shoulder to his cheek at the same time. "Listen, if you don't want to do this my way, then just give me back my money, and we'll forget your involvement in the whole thing. I'll just do it myself. Now, what's it gonna be?"

Thinking for a moment, even though this went against everything he had ever learned in this business, the weight of obligation for tuition, high priced vacations, and now this new health scare, the hitman turned and picked up the unconscious man lying on the freshly acid-stained floor and shoved him inside the barrel and then sealed the barrel top with its metal ring. With his right fist, he pounded once on the barrel lid as if to seal the deal.

"Ok, you're the client. Now, do you think you could give me a hand with this, or is that too much trouble?"

Patting the side of the barrel, the client smiled at the hitman and said, "No problem; no problem at all. Say, you mind me askin'? How'd you get the name Big Tuna anyways?"

Sighing at the over-asked question, he said with some restrained disgust, "Barracuda was already taken."

Back out on the lake, the client slowed the engine down to an idle as he continued to replay the events in his mind that brought him to the middle of Lake Keystone on a moonless night with a hired hitman named Big Tuna and a 55-gallon drum with an unconscious building contractor stuffed inside.

It was six weeks ago to the day that Harold called the number thumbtacked to the cork bulletin board hanging by the diner's front door. Local diners are great places to advertise a contracting business, and it's free. Just stick a business card up and wait for the calls.

Leaning in to examine the cards, Harold was amazed at what people did for a living. There were the obvious ones: yard work, babysitting, and boat storage. But it was the unobvious ones that drew his attention.

> **Professional Cat Sitter**
> **9 Years Experience**
> **Call 1-800-55LITTR**

> **Betty's Beauty Barn**
> **& Bakery**
> *The place for pedicures and petit Fours*
> 918-555-4321

> **Honeywagon Septic Cleaner**
> *We Never Dump on a Customer*
> Ask About Our Specials
> (918)555-7448

"Needin' someone to do some work for ya there, Harold?"

Straightening up and turning around to face the man who was leaving the diner with a toothpick in his mouth, Harold replied, "Yeah, Mitch. You got any ideas who might do good work closing in my carport?"

"Yeah, come to think of it, I do. I was talkin' to ol' Widow Anderson last week, and she told me of a fella that redid her bathroom. She said he did a good job and that he was very reasonable," then, taking the toothpick out of his mouth and pointing with it at a card in the middle of the bulletin board, Mitch said, "That's the guy right there. You might wanna give him a call."

Stabbing the bright lime green card in the middle of the bulletin board with his index finger several times, Harold mused with skepticism, "This guy right here?"

> **Mike's Mayham Construction**
> I make small projects big and
> big projects small.
>
> Call 918-555-1932

"Hey, I'm just tellin' ya what she said. Call her and ask her. Well, I gotta get to work. See ya later, Harold."

"Yeah, see ya, Mitch," Harold said over his shoulder as he pocketed the lime green card with a bit of skepticism.

"Hello, ya got Mike here. What can I do for ya?"

"Yeah, my name's Harold, Harold Pritchard, and I got your number from the bulletin board down at the diner, and I was wonderin' if you might be interested in giving me a bid to close in my carport for an office and bathroom?"

"Be happy to do that, Mr. Pritchard. I'm workin' local today close to the diner. Why don't cha give me an address, and I'll swing by on my way home this evening and take a look at it. Will that work?"

"Yeah, that'll work great. I live out here at Lake Keystone, not too far from the diner. I'm the first house on the right when you turn left on Oakwood Lane. You familiar?"

"Yeah, I know the area. See you around six, Harold."

Harold immediately felt suspicious when the dirty white '88 Ford F150 filled with roofing material pulled into the driveway. He knew instinctively he should have asked more questions on the phone and gotten more references for this guy. But it was too late for that now. He thought at least he could get a starting bid and then ask around for other bids.

Before the contractor even stepped completely from the pickup, he was talking at a rapid rate and non-stop too. "You, Harold? Man, you got a great place here! Bet you see lots a babes out on the lake from here," Mike said, pointing to the lake from the carport overlooking the water below. "Yes, sir, that's quite a view. You ain't gonna close that up, are you? I see custom-made to order windows keeping all this open. And I gotta guy who can give us a deal on windows for some free advertisement. Yeah, this can be quite a room if we keep the view. So, tell me, what did ya have in mind? What are ya thinkin', Harold?"

"Well," Harold responded a little awkwardly to this man with no boundaries on first-time meetings, "I was just wanting to close the room in, but keeping the view…you know, I hadn't thought of that view till now." Turning toward the opening and looking out over the lake, Harold mused over the possibilities. "Yeah, I don't wanna lose that view."

And with that, the contractor set the hook.

Putting his hand on Harold's right shoulder and leaning in close to his left ear, Mike spoke in intoxicating tones as he waved his hand slowly over the view, painting the picture, "Just think…coming out here in the morning with your coffee and watching the world come alive or watchin' it go to bed with a cold beer. Maybe a big screen on that wall for the game. Havin' your buddies here for poker, and a bathroom, so no need to go inside the house and bother the misses. Yeah, can you see it? Your own private man-cave. Whattaya think there, Skipper?"

Harold was startled by the closeness of Mike in his ear, but the contractor had drawn Harold's imagination into a world of possibilities. He wasn't interested in a man-cave so much as he wanted a place for all his books. And maybe a room for listening to his ever-growing jazz collection. Watching the sunset with a good book, a glass of wine, and Coltrane playing in the background, now that did sound like a place he longed to have.

Moving away from the stale breath of the contractor in his ear and turning to face him, Harold asked, "What would closing this room in with windows overlooking the lake and a full bath run me? I imagine that might go for a pretty penny."

Smiling while making a clicking sound with his tongue against the inside of his mouth, Mike said as he pointed a finger at Harold, "You'd be surprised. Let me do a little measurin' real quick, and I can give you some idea there, Skipper."

Harold was beginning to get annoyed with Mike referring to him as "Skipper," but he stepped back toward the open area facing the lake and thought there's no way this could come in under ten or maybe even twenty thousand dollars. He sighed as the new dream began to fade because he was sure he was not willing to pay that much. In fact, the more he thought about it, the more he realized why he had put this off for so long. The thing is, you see, Harold could afford it. It's just that Harold didn't like turning loose of the money. That kind of money would eat into his retirement, and he and his wife, Judy, had always wanted to go to Europe before they got too tired to travel. The more he thought of it, the more he suspected Judy would never go for it. He wished she were here right now to keep him practical, but instead, she had gone out to see her grandkids for the summer. Probably not a good idea to do this without her. He figured he'd call her later tonight and admit his folly.

Still, Coltrane and a good Cabernet Sauvignon. Hmmm.

"Well, this is just a rough estimate, you understand, but I think

I could do this right around six thousand, that's with materials and labor. Now that's just a minimum, you understand, but doable if we just do the basics. Whattaya think there, Skipper?"

Turning to Mike, Harold responded in disbelief, "What? Did you say six thousand? We're talking about a complete closing in with windows? Six thousand sounds kinda low." Harold regretted that last comment, but there was no way this carport could be closed in for that amount of money. No way!

Looking around in the growing darkness, Mike mused and nodded his head at the same time, muttering with his lips closed tightly and pursed out, "Uhum, uhum, yeah, it's doable if we're careful. Mind you, I don't cut corners, but I know some guys what owe me, and this might just be the time for them to pay off. Whattaya say? You want me to come back tomorrow in the daylight and run a more accurate cost? Be happy to do it."

Excited about the possibilities, Harold mustered an objective tone, "Well, I'd have to talk it over with my wife, but tomorrow morning would be good. What time?"

"Right after coffee at the Pick It Quick. Say around eight o'clock? That ain't too early for ya, is it? I know you lake people like to start the day slowly," Mike said with a laugh.

Perturbed with Mike's suggestion of being a late riser, Harold nodded and replied, "Yeah, eight o'clock is fine. We can do it earlier if you like. I'll be up."

"Nah, eight it is. You see, Jenny down at the Pick It Quick puts on a fresh pot of coffee at seven-thirty every morning, and that gives me time to get fresh myself. You know what I mean there, Skipper?" Mike said with a wink and a click of his tongue inside his mouth.

Annoyed with this crude man, Harold decided to ask with a smirk, "Say one last question? Why do you call your company

Mike's Mayhem Construction? Is it reflective of how things turn out?"

Chuckling, Mike smiled broadly, "It's what they call a business tactic. People immediately think the worst, but they can't help themselves, and they call me. But look at my card; most people don't. It's Mayham, not Mayhem. It's an a, not an e. It's May—ham, not May—hem. Get it? You'd be surprised how many folks get it wrong, but it does bring me business. Pretty clever, huh? Well, I'll see ya in the mornin', Skipper." Stepping into his truck, Mike stood up on the side running board and looked once more out over the lake view, "Man, what a view!" Then hopping in the cab and cranking the engine with a puff of black smoke, he drove off with "Sweet Home Alabama," blaring out into the tranquility.

Harold woke earlier than usual. Walking out to the carport with his coffee, he set up a lawn chair in front of the opening he imagined would be his study. He sat down, careful not to spill the coffee, and smiled at the glowing sunrise over the lake. Judy had told him last night over the phone if the guy could do it in six thousand or less, then do it, surprising Harold. He took a sip of the hot beverage and smiled. He loved the way Judy stood up with him on these ventures. She never hesitated when he suggested they buy this lake house many years before retirement. She said they'd work it out somehow. And now she's okay with closing in the carport, although she did say she could see her own space carved out next to Harold's. He agreed.

The four-week project was now into its sixth week. The six thousand dollar pricetag was long gone. So was the ten. Now Harold had to admit he had added a few things, well, maybe more than a few things. But Mike never tried to talk him out of it. In fact, some of the nicer things that were added, if you really thought about it, were Mike's suggestions, but Harold said he wanted that all along. It was the unforeseen things that really ran the price tag up and the time as well.

Things like the day that Mike hired a friend of his to do the plumbing. Mike said all they had to do was tie into the existing sewer line that ran under the carport slab.

"No problem there, Harold. All we gotta do is jackhammer through this here concrete a few inches and then glue on the line to your toilet. Piece a cake. Done it a million times. It'll cost a little extra 'cause we didn't calculate the line ran under the slab, but it's gotta be done. You'll be happy in the long run. Trust me."

"Shit, man! Hey, Mike, come look at this. This ain't good. I ain't never seen nuthin like it before. They got a two-inch line where it should be a four. Someone screwed up big time. We gonna have to rip all that out or run a whole separate line. This ain't never gonna pass code."

Turning back to Harold, "Don't worry about a thing there, Skipper," Mike said, grinning as he placed his hand on Harold's shoulder. "I can fix this. Like I said, it might cost a bit more than we originally thought, with the extra materials and labor and all. And we may have to grease an inspector, but I know someone; for some extra foldin' money to spend at the casino, he'll pass anything. But I ain't lying; it'll probably set us back a bit."

"Holy crap! Mike, come out here and take a look, would ya! You ain't gonna believe what they done here at the septic tank."

Looking down into the hole his plumber had just dug to view the septic line going into the septic tank, Mike just shook his head as he did a mental calculation of the time and materials it would take to repair this problem as well. He looked back at Harold through the windowless opening—the windows came in the wrong size and were now on backorder—and he could tell Harold was at the end of his limit for patience. If something didn't go his way soon, Mike figured Harold would fire the lot of them or worse.

Speaking to his plumber, Mike declared, "Well, that's a problem for another day. It's almost five, and I gotta swing by the house to get my bowling ball for league practice tonight."

Leaning in through the windowless opening, Mike smiled at Harold and said, "Listen, it's quittin' time, and I got practice tonight, so we're gonna knock off a bit early and hit it fresh in the morning. Don't worry about this latest snag. I think I can fix it without too much trouble and get ya goin' here pretty soon. Say you mind if I leave that fifty-five gallon barrel here? It freaks the folks out down at the alley with that red dangerous chemicals label on it. I use it to throw trash in. I'll just put it over here behind the carport where no one will see it. Ok, see ya tomorrow, Skipper."

Every day it seemed a new problem would develop. Harold began to wonder constantly about his sanity in starting this project. He was wishing he had some way of washing his hands of it and starting over. One thing for certain, he thought, and that is he would not have hired Mike's Mayham Construction for the job. He really could see now why folks would think of Mayhem instead of Mayham.

Judy was beginning to worry about the money. She worried

even more about Harold. He was not thinking rationally. There was no telling what he might do. Every night at dinnertime, when he would call, there was a litany of charges with extreme consequences he would roll out against the mayhem. Judy knew her husband was not prone to fits of anger or violence; however, she had never seen him this enraged. Who knew what her husband was capable of, if pushed hard enough?

Harold's stomach was beginning to build an ulcer, he was certain. He woke up every morning dreading going out into the unfinished room to watch the sun. His summer was slowly slipping away. It would not be long before he would have to get back to teaching at the university. One of the nice things about living out here at the lake was during the summers, he felt like he was already retired. But now, every day the sun came up, he was losing that feeling, and he began to wonder if he was ever getting it back. Each day meant another thousand dollars, it seemed. He had to talk to somebody, so he decided to drive over to see Widow Anderson.

"Would you like some cream with that coffee?"

"No, thanks, Wid—Ms. Anderson."

"It's Mrs. Anderson. I don't go in for all that new-fangled way of addressing folks. Now, tell me again, dear, just what your problem is with that nice young man. Why, I just can't believe he is capable of such things. He did such a nice job with my bathroom. Would you like to see? You just come back here and look at what he did."

"Now, I'll admit it did cost me a bit more than he originally figured. I was initially skeptical like you, but that was because of the issues he found in my walls and under the floor. But he saved me from future costly repairs. Like he said, it couldn't be helped. And naturally, it did cost me a little more, but just look at it. Isn't it beautiful?"

Harold had to admit the end result was certainly well done. It appeared Mike had indeed managed to pull it all together in the end. Maybe Harold thought he was being a bit premature and irrational. Things do happen, things that no one could foresee.

Then suddenly, she lowered her voice as she looked cautiously from side to side and coaxing Harold close with her index finger, she whispered, "Now, dear, it's none of my business, but if you think that you are being taken advantage of or mistreated, my great-nephew knows a gentleman back up North. He's sort of a fixer of problems, if you know what I mean," she said with a wink. "I had a problem with a neighbor next door who was always blowing his grass into my yard when he mowed. I spoke with him several times, and it seemed it just got worse and worse. Danny, that's my great-nephew, and his family were down for a visit, and he said he knew a guy that could take care of it for me. Why it wasn't more than a few days, and do you know that neighbor up and moved away. I say, moved away. I haven't seen him since Danny told me he'd take care of it. The problem just went away. I think I got that gentleman's number somewhere. Here, here it is. He lives in New Jersey, but I think he travels a lot."

"You think it's the motor?" Big Tuna said, leaning over the stern while holding a flashlight for Harold.

"Yeah, it could be she ain't getting enough fuel. I had that carburetor worked on a month ago, but I haven't really put it to the test 'til tonight. I don't think she's gonna start, and we don't need to get caught out here with this barrel on board. Let's get it overboard, and then we'll figure out what to do."

Both men leaned the barrel to one side as they lifted it toward the port side of the boat. A low moan could be heard from inside. Setting the barrel back down, Big Tuna pulled his Beretta 92-S. Three quick shots into the side, and all was quiet again out on the lake. This immediately pissed Harold off as he jumped back away from the barrel. He wanted the contractor to suffer by drowning. Locking eyes with the big hitman, he realized he was no match for this professional. Besides, Tuna was still holding the gun. Harold decided to let it go.

Again they lifted the barrel and carefully tipped it over into the dark water and watched as the bubbles marked its slow descent into hopefully forever.

"Try it again," Harold hollered at Big Tuna, who was stationed at the helm while Harold worked the gas pump.

"Well, shit! It looks like she's gonna need towed in tonight. This ain't never happened to me before. She's always started. Guess it's time to put 'er back in the shop. I'll just call my neighbor, Luther. He's a night owl, always up 'til two or three. Won't be no problem gettin' him to come tow us in."

Without looking at Harold, the hitman said low and deliberate, "Are you sure you want to do that?"

"Well, you got any other suggestions, bub?" But after saying that, Harold felt the eyes of the hitman on him even in the darkness. He felt his flippancy was pressing his luck.

They waited in the dark of the night, silently rocking back and forth on the water. The wake was picking up, and you could hear the slapping of the water against the hull. The big hitman was beginning to regret taking this job when in the distance, he heard the low rumble of an inboard diesel engine. He felt he was way outside his well-kept plans. Vaguely a light could be seen in the distance along with the engine noise. As the boat drew closer, Big Tuna could see it looked like a mini-tugboat. In fact, it was an 18 foot 1999 Bradenton Mini Tug. Clever idea for a lake boat and somewhat fortuitous, he thought at this moment. As the bow light from the tug shone ahead on the water, the hitman noticed something bobbing low on the surface of the lake. Thinking that it might be a log or some other form of debris, he slapped Harold on the shoulder and pointed to the object that the tug seemed oblivious to. It was then with horror that the hitman realized the object was the barrel. It somehow had managed to float to the surface and was in the ongoing path of the mini tug.

The effort to shout and wave Luther off his chosen path was fruitless, and the collision seemed preordained. The sturdy tug hardly recognized the object, pushing the barrel down with its hull only to have it bob up again into the propeller. There was a low, grinding, metallic sound as the propeller severed the metal retaining ring and spilled its contents on the dark surface of the lake. Luther reacted quickly to the sound and put the boat in reverse, which allowed the propeller to mangle the barrel's contents. Flustered and realizing he needed to stop and see just what it was he had run over, Luther thought he shifted the engine into neutral and leaned over the stern with a flashlight to see what he had hit.

"HOLY SHIT!" Luther screamed into the lake's dark quiet. "I've run over a body in the water, and it's stuck in my prop!" he yelled in panic to the other boat. "What'll I do Harold, what'll I do? Holy shit! We've got to get the police! Hooolly shit!"

Moving quickly to the starboard side of the bow and leaning over, Luther spasmed violently as he retched his fear and disgust into the lake. The panic in his voice was quite noticeable to Harold, but to the hitman, it was a problem with only one solution. He slowly raised his gun.

"Luther, throw me a line, and I'll pull us together. Luther! You hear me? Get it together and throw me a line," Harold spoke with a firm but even tone in hopes his neighbor would comply before they drifted any further apart and a line couldn't be tossed. If Luther missed the opportunity, then he would have to put the engine in drive, and Harold knew he would not be able to do so, not with the body still stuck in the propeller.

"LUTHER!"

Looking up toward the sound coming from in front of the boat's bow, Luther's mind begins to comprehend what was being asked of him. He moved slowly with one hand tightly gripping the rail while searching with the flashlight for the bowline with the other. Locating the rope, he let go of the rail. The movement of the boat on the water caused him to give way to his stability, and Luther fell backward, throwing the rope through the cabin's opening landing on the throttle. He retched over and over again. The silent sound of pop pop pop came from behind Harold. He saw Luther's head jerk up toward him, and then his entire body just collapsed on the deck, pulling the rope and engaging the throttle.

Turning to the hitman in terror, Harold yelled, "What the hell did you shoot him for? He wouldn't have said nothing. My God, man, he was my neighbor!"

Looking from Luther to Harold while still holding his pistol, Big Tuna said quietly, "He was going to bring some heat; heat we don't need." Raising the gun, he continued, "I told you I didn't like this plan. I told you this was not an efficient way to kill someone. I told you I couldn't afford no screwups."

BAM! Without warning, the mini tug freed itself from the body stuck in the prop by severing it in half, and the boat lunged forward into the Runabout. Both men were knocked off their feet and thrown into the dark waters. The mini tug continued to push the Runabout until it lifted the boat out of the water and capsized it with its hull now facing up on the lake waters. The tug pushed the boat to one side and then continued its course into the black night until its engine could no longer be heard.

Kicking up instinctively from beneath the surface, Harold emerged gasping for air but unable to distinguish anything due to the dark water and the darkness of the night and the fact that his uncut hair had temporarily blinded him. Turning this way and turning that, he treaded water for a few minutes before he spotted the upturned Runabout and began to make his way toward the boat's belly. Clinging to the side, Harold began to holler for the hitman.

"Tuna. Big Tuna, where are you? TU—!" Just then, a large, strong hand clamped over Harold's mouth and pulled him under the water momentarily. Popping back to the surface and spitting out a belly full of lake water, coughing and sputtering, Harold turned in the darkness, momentarily blinded again but recognizing the big man's form next to him, also clinging to the side of the upturned boat.

"You want to hold it down there, Harold. Your voice carries across the water more than you think."

"Sorry. Man, we're in a fix. We can't upright the boat, and the sun will be up in a few hours. I don't think I can swim that far to shore. Can you?"

"Let me think. Ok, here's what we're gonna do. I'm gonna swim to the tug over there that's beached on the other shore. I'm gonna take it back to the dock and disappear. You, you're gonna hang on to this boat until someone finds you when the sun comes up. You tell them you were boating at night and hit something that flipped the boat. As far as your neighbor goes, you don't know nothing since you were on the lake last night. Got it? 'Cause if you don't, I'll know. And then you'll know I know," the big man said as he pushed off into the darkness of the water. In a few moments, he was out of sight, but a voice could be heard clearly saying, "and don't call me again, ever."

A week later, Harold was sitting in his nearly-finished room in the early morning sun, starring out his new window surrounded by his books and listening to Coltrane while sipping his morning coffee. Judy was due home in two days. The semester started in a week. The police were convinced that the disappearance of Harold's neighbor was just that—a disappearance. The contractor's disappearance was also a mystery, but many thought he skipped town due to some shady dealings with a customer and the paying off of an inspector.

Harold knew that his mornings and evenings were going to be just about perfect from now on. Retirement couldn't come soon enough. While listening to a previously unreleased copy of Blue World by Coltrane, Harold began to become meditative, starring out at a solitary boat and skier on the placid lake water. Suddenly the skier was airborne as if something in the water had ejected him like a ski ramp. Leaning in with curiosity, Harold examined the scene with his binoculars. After swinging around to pick up the skier, the people in the boat appeared to be wrestling an object out of the water and into the boat.

It looked like a blue barrel.

III

Go West, Young Longhair, Go West

When I first came to Oklahoma, I was wearing overalls.

About a month before, I had stopped off in a Brigadoon foggy mountain town in Tennessee to see this beautiful lady with long blonde hair I had met the summer before. I thought an awful lot of her and really wanted to settle down and end my wanderings. With a woman like that, I really believed that it was possible, but it seems it was not to be. You see, first, there were these men from a so-called gentlemen's social club who asked me to move along and to take my dog and foreign car with me. Not sure they were fans of my longhaired ways, my bandana-wearing German Shepherd, or else they didn't like beach bums driving VWs with driftwood bumpers. And if that was not reason enough, it seems my lovely lady's ex-husband and former guest of Tennessee's penal system was gunning for me. Literally.

The guy let it be known around town that he wanted the longhair gone, and it seems he flashed a gun to show he meant business. Pretty literal, huh! Now I mentioned to the blonde-haired lady that I had never met her ex before, and since I was not the only stranger in town, how could he possibly recognize me? But it turns out—as she informed me—that I was the only longhair in town and the only one who drove a VW. I was not hard to miss in this shorthaired Smokey Mountain community.

Guess it was time for me to wander again.

Since my wanderings had planned to take me to Oklahoma to see my sister, I had asked the lovely lady what she knew about the state and possibly what they wore out there. You see, I figured it was time I learned to blend in—being different no longer seemed to be to my advantage. She thought, based on a documentary she had recently watched on PBS, that most Okies wore overalls.

"You know, the kind you see on men from the dust bowl days," she said.

So, we headed to the local Ace Hardware store in downtown Sweetwater to peruse their selection of Oklahoma-blending-in overalls. After rummaging through their two-brand selection, I purchased a pair of Big Smith Railroad Style Hickory Stripe Denim with the trademarked bib pocket design. To complete the ensemble—remember I was trying to blend—I borrowed a bandana from my faithful companion, Emmylou, thinking that I really would look the part as someone who had grown up as a "goat roper" in the red dirt state and who was possibly boyhood friends with Woody Guthrie. The truth is, if you took one look at me, you'd think I was more the type to be friends with Woody's son, Arlo.

Now I'm from South Florida, and wearing a shirt is considered formal attire for a date that involves dining-in. So, one early foggy morning, I took off from Tennessee wearing my Big Smith overalls, no shirt, Kino sandals, and a red bandana tied around my neck. Yes sir! I truly looked like a native Okie, driving my '71 dark green VW Beetle with driftwood bumpers and a German Shepherd dog hanging out the passenger window with her own blue bandana tied as always around her neck.

Oklahoma, here we come.

My first stop was at a 76 Truck Stop just outside of Nashville to fill up with pushin' water. When I went to pay the man inside the lobby, he hollered at me, saying I couldn't come in without a shirt on. Cursing, he pointed to the red-lettered sign posted by the double glass doors. It read:

NO SHIRT
NO SHOES
NO SERVICE!

"Cain't you read the damn sign, hippie?"

I hollered back that I just wanted to hand him the money for the gas and wasn't planning on coming into the restaurant to eat. He still said I wasn't coming in without putting on a shirt. Guess I was feeling scrappy, so I just threw the money on the lobby floor and headed back to my car. All of a sudden, I panicked, realizing the possibility that this protesting action would likely assemble the local gentlemen's social club. I took off in a sprint to the car. Man, I wished at that moment I had taught Emmylou to start the car! I could see it now—the morning headlines would read: "Longhair Found Hanging from Tree; Possibly from Oklahoma." So, I jumped into the Beetle, and me and Emmylou took off as fast as the car would go. Emmylou wondered why the hurry as she stared at me with those dark brown eyes and concerned whine, but then turned to take advantage of the wind blowing quickly past her nose and the sight of the trees going by faster than usual.

Normally, Emmylou and me would just pull over to a roadside park and sleep on a picnic table, but with the thought that they might be chasing us, I just kept driving. We pulled off the first I-40 exit to Shawnee around midnight that evening, and feeling safe finally, followed the signs to the campus of Oklahoma Baptist University, where my sister attended. It was too late to call and have her put me up, so I found a parking lot for used cars at a dealership and parked amongst them, hoping no one would notice. Emmylou and I lay the seats back so that we were out of sight of anyone driving by. I hoped the night would hide the driftwood bumpers.

Morning found us parked outside Benton's Café in downtown Shawnee for breakfast. We arrived there on the recommendation of an early morning salesman to the car lot who was eager to meet his weekly quota. He said he hadn't seen me when he closed the night before.

"Welcome to Oklahoma," he hollered as we drove out of the parking lot, pointing the way to downtown.

Emmylou decided to wait outside on the sidewalk keeping vigil over the VW as was her custom. Benton's, it turns out, is a local favorite that has been around since 1949, according to the pictorial history on the walls. And according to an old man at the register, they put on a good breakfast.

I was greeted by a woman who looked hard enough to be in her sixties but moved like it was her prom. Her hair was dark with random runs of gray, and her eyes of deep brown saw every motion, every shrug, every nod of the chin making their requests for more of this and less of that. It was as if this were her orchestra, and she was the maestro. Everyone respected her leadership and leaned in for their cues.

"Mornin' and welcome to Benton's. My name's Wanita. Have

a seat anywhere, hon. What can I get ya ta drink? Coffee?" she asked as she spun around and surveyed the diners' needs and then moved to meet them while dancing through the tables and sashaying with the chairs and making her way to the coffee pot.

Choosing a table near the window so I could keep an eye on Emmylou, I replied as if I had been accepted into this breakfasting family, "Coffee would be fine."

"You take cream or sugar, hon?" she asked without turning back.

"Nah, just coffee."

And she continued the dance.

Pouring my coffee, she asked, "You know what you want, or do you need a menu?" Wanita used neither pencil nor pad. This lady was a true veteran.

"Do you know how to make a decent bowl of grits in this place?"

Now, in hindsight, this was probably not how I should have started with Wanita. She proceeded to tell me that the Native American Folk was makin' grits long before I was even a stirring in my daddy's pants or his daddy or his daddy before him. She then leaned in close with her both hands on the table, and fixing her eyes on mine, she spoke slow and clear with the smell of cigarettes on her breath:

"And if you don't like my grits, then...you can go back there in the damn kitchen and make 'em yourself. But I'd be careful what you say to the cook." Then she winked and, with a smile, turned quickly on her left foot and hollered to the cook through the serving window, "Bowl of grits! And make 'em good. We got us a connoisseur out here."

Everyone laughed along with Wanita.

Wanita returned to her ballet through the throng of tables,

pouring coffee and offering advice on local politics or an expected quip accompanied with a smile or wink. She knew everyone and everyone joshed with her and her verbal jabs. She was the matriarch of this family of difference. There were businessmen and construction workers and college students, and folks from the reservation, all in various colors, sizes, and economic levels. And she even included an out-of-town beach bum with long hair and no shirt under his attempted costuming overalls. I thought at that moment the world could use more Wanitas. I knew that I could.

"You ain't from around here, are ya hon'?" Wanita remarked with a smile as she placed a generous bowl of steaming grits in front of me. The cook knew his way around grits. A big glob of butter graced the center of the bowl.

"I'm from South Florida. Me and Emmylou came to see my sister at OBU," I replied while tapping the window with my thumb toward the vigilant dog lying next to the VW.

"Whew! Now that's somethin' ya don't see every day," she offered as she strained her neck to look out the front window over the café curtains. "Hon' don't cha know that tree limbs is for the fireplace and not for car bumpers?" Wanita exclaimed as she turned to the others in the dining room and brought their attention to what was parked out by the curb with the nodding of her head toward the outside. The rest of the patrons expectedly stood and stretched their necks to look out the window to the sight. Signaling the others to join in with her motherly laugh and a wink of the eye, she patted me gently on the top of my head as if to say: That's nice, son, now take that back outside as any mother would do when her son offers her a snake he proudly found in the grass.

I suddenly knew this could be home even without a shirt on.

Turning right onto North Kickapoo and then left onto University Street, I took the first right onto the oval drive and drove past the fountain and the buffalo statue—painted green by graduating seniors, according to an annual tradition. I found a parking spot right in front of a dorm called Montgomery Hall on the northwest side of the oval that had a column patio area for sitting outside. A lone girl was sitting reading as I pulled in and shut off the engine. I told Emmylou to wait as I hopped out of the car, quickly tugging on my red bandana to make sure it looked natural. As I approached, she looked up from her book and said without enthusiasm, "You must be Debbie's brother from Florida."

My first thought was that my reputation preceded me, and I needed to remember to thank my sister for passing on such an obviously wonderful description of her brother. I should have just smiled and left the perceived compliment with my ego, but I couldn't help myself, so hooking my thumbs in the overall shoulder straps and bending from the waist toward her, I asked, "So, what have you heard, babe?"

She replied at first without looking up, "Oh, I ain't heard nothing," and then looking up slowly and directly into my eyes, she continued, "Debbie just said to be on the lookout for the strangest lookin' guy you'd ever seen, and that would be her brother." And leaning her head around me to look into the parking lot, she continued, "She also said you'd be drivin' a Volkswagen and have a big, blonde shepherd ridin' with you."

Then sitting back up straight and looking me directly in the eyes again, she said with a smile that was meant to show that I was not the first one to flirt with her, "You are MJ, aren't you?"

I'm guessin' my blendin' needs a rethink.

After shattering my ego, the girl directed me to the Kerr

dormitory, where my sister was staying for the summer. Well, folks, I ain't used to the rules and regulations of private Baptist colleges in the Midwest. Still, I figured folks here would be pretty friendly and accepting of anyone who looked like they used to belong here. After all, Wanita had made me welcome.

Not so.

Immediately someone started hollering, "Man on floor! Man on floor!"

Now, normally my first reaction would be that the ladies of Oklahoma were happy to see a real live beach bum dressed in their native attire, but my recent experience with the "Welcome to OBU" girl told me otherwise. I quickly got the impression that it was a warning to virginal Baptist girls to swallow the keys to their chastity belts and then to bolt their doors and hide in their closets. However, that morning I learned that not all Baptist girls had intentions of swallowing keys and bolting doors due to the amount of bras and panties that seemed to be posed before the slowly delayed closings of open doors.

A slight woman with prison guard eyes came out of an office to my left and asked firmly and without courtesy, "Is there something I can help you with?" She paused and looked me over real slow as she pointed to the door, "Men are not allowed in the dorm without an escort. Now please leave, and, for goodness sake—put a shirt on!"

Backing up, I explained I was Debbie's brother who had come for a visit and would she mind informing her I was here. And then, after bumping into the doorway backward, I decided it was best and safer to wait outside.

That was only the first hint that Oklahoma had some strange ways of doin' things.

Several days later, I would go with my sister to a Baptist church camp—I guess she was worried about my wicked ways—anyways, she told me the camp was in the mountains with waterfalls and lots of wildlife, and they had a pool. Pools are good. It's like the beach with jetties on four sides to keep the bikinis all together. When I heard the announcement that it was time for the girls to go swimming, I grabbed my baggies and towel and headed to the pool. The lifeguard stopped me at the gate and told me that the boys swam later in the day and that this time was for the girls only.

"Exactly! Why would I want to swim with a bunch of guys? Hell, I'm from South Florida, and I think the idea of separating the girls from the boys cuts down on the competition. Don't know why we don't do this back home."

He strongly suggested I attend chapel services that night.

On the front steps of Kerr Hall, my sister greeted me. "Well, brother, it looks like you sure stirred things up. The whole dorm is talkin' about you. You know you're going to have to put a shirt on. They won't let you in anywhere out here without a shirt. Where's Emmylou?"

After visiting for a couple of hours, I told Debbie I wanted to head back downtown to explore the cultural sights. She told me where to meet up for supper and then admonished me to be careful, "this ain't Florida."

I noticed a black and white behind me as I down-shifted through an intersection. Immediately he threw on his lights and gave me a couple of blasts from his siren as I pulled over to the curb. It may not be Florida, but the hassle is the same.

"What can I do for you, Officer?"

Reaching up with his middle finger, he lowered his sunglasses and leaned in close to the open window. "You ran through a stoplight back there at the intersection."

Turning around and sticking my head out of the window, I looked back at the space over the middle of the intersection and remarked with amazement, "Officer, I hate to be the one to inform you, but there ain't no stoplight hangin' in the middle of that intersection. Somebody musta stole it."

Standing up slowly and pushing his sunglasses back up on his nose, he calmly replied, "We put the light on the corner of the intersection," pointing with his finger. "Everybody around here knows that." Then looking from one end of the VW to the other, he said slowly, "But you ain't from around here, are you?"

Man! I was beginning to think that the lovely blonde lady back in Tennessee got the state wrong in that special she saw. My attempt at blending wasn't workin' at all.

"No, sir. I'm here visitin' my sister at OBU. Just in town for a week or so. By the way, most folks put their stoplights hangin' from the middle of the intersection. It's a universal rule, I think. How do you expect out-of-towners to know about them lights ifn' you set them on the street corner?"

Almost as if he forgot all about my suggestion to rethink stoplight placement, he walked slowly around the car and shook his head when he looked down at the driftwood bumpers.

"Where'd you get them bumpers?"

"Found 'em on a beach back home. Pretty cool, huh?"

"Listen," he said as he leaned back in the window and lowered his glasses again, "Seeing's how you are just visitin', I'm only gonna warn you." Then as he turned back toward his car, he said over his shoulder, "And put a shirt on!"

After spending time with one of Shawnee's finest, I headed to the park for some Frisbee with Emmylou. I thought it interesting that the cop hadn't hassled me further. Back home, I would not have gotten away without a full pat-down and a tossing of my car. Maybe cops everywhere ain't all the same.

I headed back to the university to meet Debbie and her boyfriend. Pulling into the parking lot of apartments where Debbie worked as an RA, I saw her boyfriend pulling up at the same time. I also noticed another cop pulling in behind me. Emmylou must have noticed him too because she jumped out of the window and ran to greet him. I figured after the good experience at the traffic light, she wanted to thank him and any fellow officers for not hassling her human. He looked like one of those rent-a-cops used for security. He was long past retirement age, and clearly, he kept the local donut shops open. I noticed in the rearview mirror he was concerned about an unleashed German Shepherd running toward him. He yelled at me to call my dog off. He was adamant and repeated the order multiple times.

"Call your dog off! Call this damn dog off, or I'll put it down!"

He was attempting to pull his gun all this time but was having trouble releasing the thumb strap. Emmylou was circling him and barking her thanks, not caring about the man's fright. At this time, Debbie's boyfriend, hearing the commotion, came running from his car to intervene in the situation, yelling, "Don't shoot! Don't shoot! She's not going to hurt you. Stand still! Just stand still, and she'll calm down."

It was then I realized the seriousness of the situation and that Emmylou's appreciation dance was not being appreciated. I joined in the verbal protest, yelling as I ran to the ruckus, "Don't shoot! Emmylou, be still! Please, don't shoot my dog!"

Whether it was my command to be still or Emmylou's realization that this cop was not grateful for all her attention, she just sat down and looked back to me and then to the cop and then to the boyfriend. The cop finally cleared his holster, but instead of pointing his gun at Emmylou, he was pointing it at the screaming longhair running toward him.

"STOP, OR I'LL SHOOT! On your knees, hands locked behind your head! NOW!"

"Officer! Don't shoot that one either! He ain't from around here. He doesn't know to wear a shirt. Please, don't shoot him; his sister won't like it."

Kneeling there in the gravel in my Big Smith's, I thought of all the folks kneelin' in the gravel with their hands behind their heads.

And then I thought: sure could use more Wanitas right now.

IV

Burying a Cat in an Oklahoma Winter

✦

I don't really have much against cats, more of a dog person myself. Always have been. But cats, well, cats have their own way about them that can make me a bit crazy sometimes. You'll never see a dog test to see if you're willing to let them out; no, a dog says they want out, they mean, "If you don't let me out now, then you can clean it up." A cat? Now a cat will saunter over to the door and act as if they want to go out, but when you get to the door, they up and turn with their tail in the air as if to say, "Just checking to make sure you know where the door is when I am good and ready to go out."

Yeah, that makes me nuts. Or how about this? They come in and rub all over your leg as if to say, "Boy, I missed you. Let's cuddle." Then, when you bend down and give them a little scratch behind the ear, they shake their head as if they are trying to rid themselves of your scent, and meander off to find their favorite sunbeam. Damn cats.

This is a story about a cat named Bosco.

Soon after I had decided to stay in Oklahoma for a bit, I moved into a trailer with my younger sister's boyfriend. Truth is, I had to stay because the VW was acting up, and my funds were running low. So I stayed to find work to build up my travelin' money.

My ol' man fronted me the cash to split the rent on a two-bedroom trailer in a park off North Harrison Street. Initially, it was just me, Emmylou, and my sister's boyfriend, Alex. The trailer was near the bottom of the one-way-in, one-way-out road on a hill. I needed the hill for the VW. It quit starting for some reason, so I had to push it and jump in and pop the clutch anytime I had to go somewhere. Parking facing downhill just made it easier to start by myself. Every time I pushed that car off, it reminded me that I probably shouldn't have skipped Mr. Stellmacher's mechanic's class in tenth grade as often as I did.

Let me say a thing or two about Alex. I liked him the first time we met. You see, Oklahoma was not known for longhairs at that time unless you are a part of the beautiful indigenous folk that belonged to the land. Alex's long hair was due mostly to him being a musician. He drove a white 1965 Plymouth Fury four-door sedan with a dented front fender. He called it the "'65 Dent." If my memory serves me right—and Alex often says it doesn't—the '65 Dent had a transmission hump that ran the length of the car from front to back. On the passenger's side, the floorboard up front was level with the transmission hump. That was due to the fact that Alex used that side of the car for his trash. I remember rummaging through it one day and found a half-eaten burger from Hamburger King. Alex remarked, "That can't be mine. I would never knowingly throw out a Hamburger King burger."

Alex was brilliant, one of those brainiac types. You know, kinda' like a human calculator or somethin'. Because of his magic with numbers, Alex had a professor that got him to teach some high-level math class he was taking so this professor could slip off to the faculty lounge for a second cup of coffee and some flirting with the girls' swim coach. They say that music is all math—guess that's why Alex was such an amazing musician. I mean, the dude could read music, write music, play any instrument, and sing like it's nobody's business. I envy that. The sixties short-circuited some of my gray cells because I can't add a simple column of figures. I break out in a cold sweat if someone asks, "What's six times nine?" But even with all those brains, Alex still had a problem sometimes doing common sense stuff, like cleaning the trash out of the car or getting homework done before it's due. I remember there was this one morning while Alex was driving to his music theory class; he was eating a burrito with one hand and scribbling with the other on the dash of the car some homework assignment he just remembered was due. Alex told me later the assignment was to rearrange a traditional Christmas hymn for the orchestra to play. The orchestra found his arrangement so difficult that he had to show them how to play the new piece. He got an A+ for the assignment, I know 'cause I found his graded paper crumbled up in the floorboard of the '65 Dent two weeks later with a half-eaten burrito wrapped inside.

Now, I know I said this was a story about a cat named Bosco, and I'm getting to that.

One night after a date with my sister, Alex came home with a bundle inside his A-2-type brown leather bomber jacket his dad had given him. To match the ensemble, Alex also wore a brown Fedora and smoked a pipe. He looked like some WWII pilot/private eye walking through a London fog. It turns out that the purring bundle in his jacket was a kitten that had come wandering up from out of nowhere and was rubbing Alex's pant leg while he was standing outside my sister's dorm, stalling for a kiss goodnight. My sister had a soft spot for anything furry and cute, so she convinced Alex to take it home since she was not allowed pets in the dorm.

"Your sister named it Bosco. It's a cat!" he said as he dropped it in front of Emmylou to see the dog's reaction.

Normally, Emmylou is like me—no real affection towards cats. But the sudden surprise of a bite-size morsel being willingly offered up must have dumbfounded Emmylou for a moment. She looked at Alex and then me to see if the late-night snack was really meant for her. Before she could react, the kitten did the unthinkable: Instead of rising up on her claws with an arched back and wide eyes and hissing, she just went over, stretched, and then laid down beside Emmylou's warm belly and went fast to sleep, continuous purring. Emmylou looked up at me as if to say, "Well, that's not fair. I can't eat it now."

The next few days were pretty difficult for Emmylou. As long as they were in the trailer, the dog tolerated the kitten. That is to say, she didn't eat it. But when they went outside, it was altogether different. You see, outside, Emmylou had a reputation to uphold. She couldn't be seen hanging with a kitten. Not only was she the new dog in the trailer park, but she was from South Florida. Oklahoma dogs took their heritage seriously. If you weren't sired by some hungry hobo mutt just passin' through or taught to swim from inside a gunny sack, you weren't really meant for this part of the country. Besides, no dog in the neighborhood believed the stories of this bandana-wearing German Shepherd, who said she could scale a six-foot-high chain-link fence or scratch through the wooden panel of an outside door while chained to and dragging an A-frame dog house made from an oak pallet with a four by eight sheet of three-quarter plywood. "Impossible!" them trailer park dogs all barked, "them Florida dogs sure can tell some tales."

The kitten kinda' grew on us. He was pretty funny to watch

when we were stoned. I imagined he was pretty funny even when we weren't stoned, but I can't remember if that ever happened. My sister gave the kitten an early Christmas present of a ball on a string. We spent hours throwing that ball and then jerking it back just out of reach when the kitten was about to pounce. If he did manage to grab it with his teeth or claws, I would shake the string, and his head or whole body would bounce up and down like he was the ball itself. You know folks is always saying cats are so damn smart and if that's so, then how come the kitten didn't just grab the string and put an end to havin' the ball jerked away? Maybe he was smart. After all, he got two longhairs to laugh every time he'd play with that ball. Eventually, the ball ended up under the couch, and the kitten never ventured after it. Emmylou wondered why. She loved watching the kitten bounce up and down.

Both Alex and I were having trouble finding work, so entertainment had to be cheap, like bouncing kittens on a string. For some reason, Oklahoma had an aversion to hiring longhairs. Alex solved his problem by buying a cheap, short gray-hair wig that made him look like Professor Irwin Corey. It looked ridiculous, but his night-shift supervisor at K-Mart said as long as he kept it on while working, the job was his. Eventually, I decided it was worth a try, so I went to the wig store. But I didn't grasp the concept quite like Alex. Guess I smoked too much weed before going. The salesgirl thought it unusual that I bought a long blonde wig for myself. It was a nice wig. Can't understand why nobody would hire me.

I did manage to find temporary work at a small Christmas tree lot that didn't mind my hair. I took Emmylou with me to keep me company on the long nights. She was also helpful when local thugs would try to relieve me of inventory. It's hard to argue with a German Shepherd whose thinking is that the trees belong to her. I also gave some thought to bringing the kitten down to the lot as a prop for sympathetic ladies looking for a last-minute tree. You never know the power of a cute kitten.

My last night working was on Christmas Eve, naturally. As a bonus, the owner told me to take a tree home if I needed one. He also threw in some used lights. After tying a scrawny tree to the roof of the VW, I pushed the car off, and me and Emmylou headed to the trailer with this symbol of American capitalism. Alex and I had planned on a Christmas dinner of chicken-fried steak sandwiches at Del Rancho. We didn't have chicken-fried steak in South Florida. It was like manna from Heaven for a skinny beachbum who had spent the first twenty-plus years deprived of this crispy delicacy. What an evening: decorating an unplanned tree with free lights and then filling our bellies with Oklahoma's finest. Christmas came early to the trailer park.

"Hey, got a tree and some lights."

"You got a tree stand?"

"Tree stand?"

We leaned the tree into a corner in the living room, but after stringing the lights, we realized the wall plug was on the other wall behind the couch. I lifted the couch while Alex ran the green extension cord with the big end for three other plug-ins underneath to the wall.

"Hey, Bosco, your ball!" he said, looking back over his shoulder to the kitten.

The kitten made note of this for later.

"Man, ain't nuthin' finer than Del Rancho's chicken-fried steak.

I'm stuffed," I said while taking one last hit on the roach we found in the ashtray of the VW. "Santa musta' left it," I told Alex when it was discovered. "Hey, did you turn the lights off?"

Before leaving, we had purposely left the tree lights on for the kitten and Emmylou to enjoy. As I unlocked the door, I reached inside to turn the trailer lights on, but they didn't come on.

Alex lit his lighter as he moved to the hallway, "Probably a fuse. Coulda' been those old tree lights. They look kinda' iffy when we strung them up." Leaning over to look out the window in the dining room, he remarked, "Yeah, I bet it's a fuse. The rest of the park has lights. Let me check."

When the lights came on, the tree lights did not. Emmylou seemed unusually excited about something, so I looked around to see if perhaps she couldn't hold it and left us a present to clean up.

I noticed the kitten was lying halfway under the couch and had the big end of the green extension cord in his mouth. Thinking he was playing, I reached down and grabbed the cord and shook it like the ball on the string. His whole body stiffly bounced up and down. He didn't let go of the big end of the cord.

"Crap!" I hollered as Alex walked back into the living room, looking around me at the kitten lying still on the floor. At the same time, we both realized Bosco's error in playing with the cord.

"Man, I was just gettin' to where I liked havin' that kitten around. Your sister's gonna be upset."

"Well, I guess we got to bury him. Have we got a shovel?"

"I seen one next door leanin' against their back steps. Don't think they'd mind us borrowing it. I'll go ask."

As Alex headed out the door, I realized that I had to get Bosco loose from the cord, and I suddenly started feeling sick with the idea. I never did like messing with things dead. Hell, I'd never even been to a funeral in my life. When it came to family pets that passed on, my dad always took care of it. I thought for a moment of seeing if Alex would mind picking Bosco up and then decided if I covered him with a towel, I could do this. I looked at Emmylou, and she laid down with her head on her front paws and looked up with her brown eyes while emitting a sad whine. Guess she, too, was gonna' miss Bosco.

Alex came in as I was laying an old beach towel gently over Bosco, and sudden emotion swept over me. I did my best to suppress it, not wanting Alex to see, but I think Emmylou knew. She got up and came over to me and nuzzled my arm with her wet nose while offering a few consolatory licks. Bosco's body was stiff, and I had to pry open his mouth to get the cord out. I lifted him gently and wrapped him in the old towel. There was a faint smell of ocean on it.

"I'll get a flashlight. Oh, and the folks next door gave us two shovels. They said we'd need them. Not sure what they meant."

Late December in Oklahoma can be pretty damn cold with the wind blowin' like it was. It was about now that I realized my CPO shirt-jacket was not meant for Oklahoma winters. Behind the trailer leading down to the railroad tracks was a patch of woods that seemed a good place to bury Bosco. There was no moon or stars out, so when we looked off in the distance, we couldn't tell where the horizon was. It's amazing how beautiful darkness can be.

"Let's get this done. I'm freezin'," Alex chattered through his teeth as he raised the shovel and drove it down hard into the dark red clay. "Shit! The ground's frozen! I can't get the shovel to dig."

"What? You're kidding! Maybe you're hittin' a rock?" I then put my foot on the shovel and pushed down as I, too, realized the ground was not going to yield. "Damn!"

"I'd forgotten how hard the clay can be here in Oklahoma. Especially in the winter," Alex said through hard breaths that were visible like smoke.

"Well, at this rate, we ain't never gonna get a hole dug. Whata' you think we ought to do? We can't just leave Bosco layin' out here all night," looking back over my shoulder at the bundle of towel laying on the frozen dirt. Emmylou had followed us and was now lying close to Bosco as if to say, "You were alright for a cat."

"Maybe we should just scrape some dirt over the top of him and put some rocks on him until morning. It's too cold to stay out here all night. My hands are freezing."

"Guess you're right," I said sadly as I bent over and began to make an effort to scrape the hard surface into some sort of semblance of dirt. The edges of the towel were still exposed when Alex came up carrying a few rocks in each hand. I helped him look, and we managed to make a covering pile.

Gathering the shovels, we headed back toward the trailer. Looking back, the darkness had accepted Bosco. Then I heard Alex exclaim, "Look, the tree lights are back on."

I wasn't sure if my tears were from the biting wind or for Bosco.

V

Closet Plants

You know, sometimes there are places that we live in that always have a special meaning in our memory. Sometimes it's a house; sometimes it's the land where the house sits; sometimes it's the people in the house; and sometimes it's the people that live near the house or people you meet while living in that house. This is a story about a house and the people who lived near that house.

I've lived in many different places over the years that I have been traveling around this beautiful country. I left south Florida and eventually settled for the hills of Oklahoma. After living in a trailer with a roommate, a dog, and a cat that we had to bury one winter, I ended up moving into a little three-room house in an alley next to an old large two-story house whose entry was in the back of the house facing the alley.

The little house I moved into had a living room that also doubled as the bedroom without any separating walls. On the wall furthest from the front door, I set up an old iron bed and dresser. The room was so small the bed actually covered over half the length of the living area. At the foot of the iron bed, I placed a blue-green, vinyl-covered couch to serve as the separation from the sleeping area and the visitin' area. Across from the couch on the wall with the front door was a small set of wooden shelves made up of 1x12s and cinder blocks with an old TV set and a collection of books by J. R. R. Tolkein and Stephen R. Donaldson. Also on the shelves was a dark brown wooden cigar box from Havana where I kept my stash and rolling paraphernalia. The vinyl couch had several rips in the material, so I covered it with an 8 x 12 48-star battleship flag I had brought with me from Florida. Over the years, the flag was misused for protesting by covering furniture, draping beds, hanging as a room separator, or just covering a wall in need of paint. My dog, Emmylou, slept on the flag-covered couch, though to my knowledge, she never openly protested the war while doing so.

Walking across the room between the couch and the shelves opposite the front door was an opening that led to the alley-like kitchen, which ran the length of the living/bedroom. Being so narrow, the stove and refrigerator both were on the same wall, along with some open shelves that served as a pantry. Opposite the stove was the back of the house with an outside door halfway down the wall. With your butt against the outside wall, you barely had room to open the oven door without hitting your knees. At one end of the kitchen was a small window and room for a table and two chairs as long as the chairs weren't placed opposite each other. I just ate on the couch.

On the other end of the kitchen was an opening to the bathroom. The bathroom must have been an afterthought because you stepped down into it, showing it had been added on later. Immediately to your right was the toilet, and in the corner right up against the toilet was the shower. Whoever built it was thinking of efficiency. They sloped the whole bathroom concrete floor toward the shower area and put a drain in the corner. There was a small window next to the shower about head level, but there was no shower curtain or even a bathroom door. Because the bath was constantly a damp environment, the towel rack was outside on the wall in the kitchen. I imagine whoever added the bath didn't have the expertise when it came to hooking up drain pipes. The drain hole around the pipe was a tad bigger on one side, thus allowing the water to run out not only the pipe itself but between the floor and the pipe under the concrete floor. This also allowed things to enter into the shower, mostly leeches. Every time I showered, I felt like Humphrey Bogart having to go back into the reed-choked water to pull the African Queen out of the swamp with Katherine Hepburn minding the rudder in the stern while wiping her brow with a lace handkerchief of the jungle sweat.

Taking a shower in this house took grit. I began the ordeal by scooping up the leeches with a metal spatula and dumping them in the kitchen trash. But after one night of that, I learned the disgusting little things crawled out and ended up in various unwanted places in the kitchen, such as an open bacon grease coffee can on the stove. So I decided the best thing to do was to flush them down the toilet. I was never certain they didn't crawl out of the septic and back into the shower. In fact, more than once, the thought of them kept me awake at night. Every once in a while, I missed one and would step on it in the dimly lit shower. The squishing feeling almost made me give up showers forever, but I thought of Bogart and got back in the water.

Opposite the shower and toilet was another opening into a closet with a sawed-off broom handle that served as a clothes rack. Where the added closet wall met the outside wall of the house was another gap. It looked like the bathroom add-on was pulling away from the house. The gap was big enough for an outside plant to grow through, and with all the moisture in the bathroom, the plant flourished with each passing season. It bloomed and flowered in the spring and dropped its leaves in the winter. And when the winds blew, it danced. Guess I could have cut it down outside and patched the gap in the wall, but I just let the plant grow since I didn't have very good luck growing house plants.

This reminded me of a time back in south Florida when Stan and I shared an apartment together. We kept a small emergency stash inside the plastic toilet paper holder, which hung on the wall near the shower curtain across from the toilet. Being guys, we figured any water that escaped the shower had soap in it; therefore, it was clean and helped to keep the floor disinfected. Our thinking was flawed, and in the corner of the wall and shower, mold began to accumulate. Evidently, a seed or two fell out of the toilet paper holder and germinated in that corner. One day as Stan was sitting on the throne, he began to yell—with great enthusiasm—for me to come and look. Like I said, we are guys, and I wasn't falling for that disgusting look down the toilet at what he had deposited. But Stan kept yelling, and finally, I went to see what all the fuss was about. Still sitting on the toilet, Stan pointed with a shaking finger while he looked at me with the proud grin of a newborn father at the little Jamaican plant growing on the floor in the mold. The plant grew to about a healthy bowl full when some visiting stoner using the toilet happened to think that this was like those fancy hotels where they leave a little chocolate mint on your pillow. Try as we might, we could never get another plant to grow after that.

One day, I happened to drive by a nursery and decided to

pull in and ask if they could identify the plant growing in my Oklahoma closet. A kind, grandmotherly woman with her long gray hair piled on top of her head and held by a number two pencil stood behind the counter. She adjusted her glasses as I came in and asked if I needed help. Explaining to her about my closet plant, she said, "It sounds like a native thistle, dear. It will put on the most beautiful purple flower during its season. They're very hardy, so you won't have to do anything since it is in the shower area and gets all that moisture. It'll pretty much take care of itself."

"Thank you. I was hoping it would survive, be-ins that it's not growin' where it's supposed to."

"Sometimes, dear, we grow where it's not natural, but we adapt."

Like I said earlier, a house can leave a lifetime of memories. And so can the people in and around that house. Next door lived two girls named Nancy and Lisa. I hadn't been settled in my new digs more than a day when they came knocking on my front door one evening. They introduced themselves and presented me with a housewarming gift of homemade brownies and a welcome to the alley, along with an invite to come to dinner the first chance I got. Gratefully receiving the brownies, I asked if they were special brownies, and they both giggled *yes*.

Smelling the warm brownies, I grinned, "Well, ain't this special, kinda like a newborn speckled pup."

They both looked at one another and then broke into laughter. "Where the hell are you from? You certainly aren't from Oklahoma," Nancy remarked.

"Nah, I'm from south Florida. Me and Emmylou are travelin' the country and decided to stay awhile in your neck of the woods."

Emmylou then wandered out to greet the new neighbors and to see if perhaps they brought her anything in the form of a "welcome to the alley" gift as well.

Again the girls looked at one another and broke into the same shared laughter.

"Well, we got to be going. We work in Tulsa, and it's a bit of a drive, so don't forget dinner one night next week. We both work until Sunday night late, so we spend the weekend in Tulsa. Plan on any night Monday through Thursday. Ok?" Lisa instructed me with a seductive smile.

As they walked to their car, I waved with my own smile and another thanks for the goodies. Then looking down at Emmylou, I remarked, "Those are some fine lookin' ladies. And look, they brought me brownies—special brownies."

Emmylou looked up with her best sad eyes and thought, "I like brownies."

As I said earlier, the shower had no curtain, and the bath had no door. Emmylou usually alerts me to someone at the front door, but if that someone knew her and gave her a scratch between the ears, calling her good girl while coming in, the alert generally never sounded. Stepping into the kitchen for my towel, I was greeted with a whistle from Nancy and a clapping of hands along with, "Nice, babe! Nice!"

Startled and somewhat embarrassed, I quickly wrapped the towel around my waist and looked sternly at Emmylou. She didn't understand the problem.

"You could've told me we had company," I said to Emmylou. "Sorry, Nancy, I didn't hear you come in."

Nancy looked down at Emmylou, and wagging her finger at her, she said sternly, "Bad dog." Then she smiled as she scratched

Emmylou between the ears.

Looking back at me, she replied without shame, "Not to worry. I let myself in without thinking. The alley tends to make me think family," she said with a sexy smile, "but don't worry; from now on, Lisa and I will be sure to announce ourselves after we come in."

Ater a moment of hesitation, she said with another smile and a wink, "Besides, it's nice to have the tables turned now and then."

At the time, I was not sure what she meant.

"Have you eaten yet?"

"No, as a matter of fact, I was just cleanin' up to go out. You and Lisa wanna come?"

"We got dinner on the stove. I just came over to see if you wanted to join us."

"Give me a couple of minutes to get some jeans on, and I'll be right over."

Turning to leave, Nancy looked back over her shoulder and said, "You can wear that towel if you want. Lisa and I won't mind." Then scratching Emmylou between the ears, she let herself out laughing as she went.

The entry to Nancy and Lisa's house was through the back door facing the alley. It was a wooden covered porch with a 2x4 railing around it except where the three wooden steps led up to the porch. There were a couple of metal lawn chairs from the 50s, painted enamel green and rusting around the arms and legs. Between them was an out-of-place small wooden crate that served as a place to put their morning cups of coffee and ashtray for their morning cigarettes. Near the metal screen door on the wall hung a mop and a broom. A dustpan leaned up against the wall underneath. The screen door had a tear, like someone had kicked it in. An attempt to repair it with duck tape to keep the bugs out was somewhat successful but not altogether secure. There were a lot of bugs stuck to the tape where it curled away from the screen. There was a porch light above the broom, inviting more bugs to the tape.

I could hear the radio blastin' from the alley, and as I approached the screen door, I saw the girls dancing and heard them singing around the kitchen to Foreigner's "Feels Like the First Time." Nancy was singing into a wooden spatula and mixing something up in a bowl at the same time. Lisa was checking on what certainly smelled good coming from the oven. I hesitated at the screen door to admire her short blue jean cut-offs.

Knocking on the door and opening it at the same time, I called out, "Hope y'all got your towels on."

Emmylou pushed past me and invited herself into the kitchen. I hadn't realized she had followed me over. "Emmylou, out! You weren't invited."

"Oh, she's ok. Let her stay," Nancy said as she scratched her between the ears. "Come on, let's eat."

Pushing the plate back for the third time, I leaned back in my chair and let out a satisfied moan of fullness and satisfaction. Emmylou was licking clean a plate Nancy placed on the floor when she thought I was not looking. I decided not to.

"Well, ladies, I didn't bring no after-dinner wine like cultured folk, but I do have this fine bit of Columbian," I declared while holding the joint up toward the old five bulb chandelier hanging over the center of the table. "Can I entice anyone to join me?"

"Fire that mother up!" Lisa said with eagerness as she began to clear the table of dishes.

In a few moments, a cloud of smoke lingered over the table, and passing the joint to Lisa, I let out a slow "Dammmmnn! That's some good shit." After a moment, I asked, breaking the stoned silence, "So, what do you ladies do for a living that has you drivin' all the way to Tulsa every weekend?"

Coughing and snorting out a repressed giggle while handing the joint to Lisa, Nancy replied, "We're strippers."

Now pot has a way of slowing one's responses down, and a reaction or an answer can seem to take a long time. After an unusually long time, I managed, "Cool!" Now any red-blooded male, upon hearing his neighbors are strippers, would certainly have managed a more enthusiastic response. But the cloud in my brain held it all in. In fact, there was a moment I thought perhaps I heard wrong and that Nancy actually said they were tippers. I had heard of cow tipping out in this part of the country, but I wasn't sure it was a real thing. But here sat two healthy women who might possibly be just that. Cow tippers. Just as I was about to inquire where they preferred to find their stock, Lisa smiled and said, "We strip in Tulsa, so the people around here don't get into our faces for what we do. Besides, my mom doesn't know I strip for a living."

Leaning over and whispering into Lisa's ear resulted in a giggling affirmation by both women. Nancy then turned to me and, leaning real close to my face, asked in a seductive whisper, "Say, would mind being our audience for some new outfits we made? You see, we make our own costumes, and it would be nice to get your opinion before we scatter them about the stage. What do you say? Dinner and a show?"

After several more joints and lots of feather boas to the face, Emmylou and I thanked our hosts and made our exit stumbling across the alley to our little house. As I opened the door, I turned and waved good night, followed by a slight bow at the waist. The girls giggled at my gallantry and blew sexy kisses across the alley at me. Mumbling to myself that no one would ever believe my night of private dancers, I crawled across the couch and fell face-first into the bed. My Joker-like smile lasted until I was unconscious.

Several days later, there was a knock at the door. Emmylou barked, so I knew it wasn't one of the girls. Besides, it was a Saturday, and they were at work.

Standing at the front door in a white short-sleeve shirt and tie was a young man who looked like he had just come from the barbershop. "How do you do? My name is Andrew. I'm the youth pastor at the First Baptist Church here in town, and we're just out visiting the neighborhood, inviting folks to come and worship with us this Sunday. We have a special speaker, and then we are providing a potluck for all our visitors. There's no charge; just come as you are." Then handing me a pamphlet with directions to the church, he said as he turned to leave, "Hope to see you there."

"Do you really mean what you just said?"

Stopping and turning around, Andrew asked, "Really mean what? That I hope to see you there. Of course, I mean that."

"No, do you really mean come as you are? Do you really hope I'll show up regardless of my attire? Or is that just some platitude you offer to put people at ease? What would you do if I showed up in cut-offs and sandals? Would you walk me down and seat me in the front row amid all the ties and freshly starched dresses? Do you really welcome everyone in your church or just those who conform to the script you play out every week?"

Walking back toward me, Andrew searched my face to see if my questions were serious and worth his time responding to, or should he just smile and offer a "God bless you" and walk away.

He decided to offer, "Our church is open to everyone. We don't discriminate. God loves everyone, so all are welcome. I mean that."

Thinking he had disarmed me, I said, "I know that God loves everyone, but do you?"

Not quite sure what he was wandering into, Andrew drew a deep breath before responding with, "You really think that God cares what you wear to church?"

"No, I don't think He minds; after all, He made us naked to start with, but I think that the folks at church would get all freaked out over how other people dress. I stopped going to church years ago cause of the script. You know the one that told you when to stand and when to sit. It told you what to sing, when to sing, and how much to sing. The script told everyone when to get out their wallets and chunk some change into the basket. Most scripts told you what the preacher was gonna preach on, and there was no changin' his mind even if God said, 'Say somethin' different.' No one deviated from the script; otherwise, they'd get done too late to beat the Methodists to the buffet."

"I don't know what you're talking about, but we don't use no script."

"You sure? You folks pass out a bulletin to everyone? Man, that's the script. Try runnin' the show without one. Guarantee nobody would know what to do. Haven't you guys ever tried just showin' up and askin' God what He wants to do that morning? Man, I bet you guys would freak out if He was to say, 'Let's just get happy and dance a bit."

Studying me hard, Andrew finally ended the conversation on his part by offering, "It don't matter to me. Come as you are is what I meant. And if God Himself wants to change the script, then so be it!" Leaning in toward me, he smiled as he offered, "Frankly, I think we could all use a little dancin' in the aisle. Come see us Sunday."

After waving his hand, he headed to the girl's house.

"They ain't home. They work weekends."

"Well, if you see them bring them along."

I smiled at the thought.

Sunday morning was beautiful. The sun was warm, and one of Oklahoma's ever-present breezes was blowing across the treetops. Stepping outside in my overalls and shirt, I took one last hit off my morning joint before flicking the roach out into the gravel driveway. I turned to encourage Emmylou to stay behind when I heard the girl's car pull up behind me.

"Whatcha all doin' home so early? Usually, it's well after dark before you get in."

Lisa responded through the open car window, "There was a scuffle out in the parking lot, and the police came, and someone started shooting, so we decided to clear out and come home early."

Coming from around the other side of the car, Nancy asked, "Where you headed all gussied up? You got a shirt on and everything."

"I'm goin' to church. You ladies want to come?"

At first, the ladies protested, saying they had no church clothes. But I quickly told them the invite was to come as you are. They both eventually agreed under the condition that I let them adorn me with a tie, seeins how I didn't own one. It was odd, but they had quite a few men's ties. I didn't ask how they came about them.

We burned another joint on the way to keep our confidence up, since the possibility existed that the ladies might know some of the crowd. I drove their car and, after parking, quickly ran around to open the door for them. I offered them my arm as we sashayed across the parking lot, me in my overalls, tie, and sandals and them in their silky miniskirts, fishnet stockings, and lots of feather boas covering up an impressive amount of cleavage.

On the way in, an obviously uncomfortable large man dressed in a tight, starched white pearl snap shirt complete with turquoise bolo tie looked twice at us and then whispered to me, "Boy, I wish I could get away with overalls and a tie." He smiled and tipped his big cowboy hat to the ladies as they giggled at the compliment. His wife grabbed him by his shirt sleeve and, with a frown, mumbled something in his ear as she drug him up the stairs and into the sanctuary.

A young teenage boy in a white shirt wearing a large red and blue striped tie that looked like it came from his father's collection was passing out bulletins. His face was full of pimples with a little peach fuzz on his upper lip. As the ladies strolled up, still arm in arm with me their escort, his mouth dropped open. Handing me a bulletin with a shaky hand, he turned to the ladies and became so self-conscious that he dropped the bulletins on the floor. Sinking to his knees, he began to mumble apologies keeping his head down so the ladies wouldn't notice the flush in his cheeks. Nancy knelt on the floor to help the poor boy and reached out and placed her hand on his arm to let him know it was all right. The boy looked up into her face and, with a pimply smile, made a silent note to confess his thoughts later.

As we entered the sanctuary, Andrew saw me and quickly made his way over to us. He led us to a prominent seat and thanked me for coming and for bringing my friends. The ladies giggled. He asked me if I got a script before coming in. I held up my bulletin, and Andrew smiled, and with a wink to me and a "ladies" to Nancy and Lisa, he was off greeting others. The ladies giggled.

I opened the bulletin and scanned the day's events. When I got to the title of the sermon, it read: "Growing Where You're Not Planted." Looking up to where I imagined God sat, I smiled up at Him as I leaned back in the pew with my hands behind my head. Turning to Nancy, I whispered, "This might not be a bad morning."

And the ladies giggled.

VI

Haulin' Glass

"He's driving a '79 White Chevy C10 pickup with a blue stripe down the side. My supervisor says he's in his early 20s, long blonde hair, round yellow-tinted glasses, and a mustache. Goes by the name of MJ. I'm not sure what his real name is. Hell, I never even met the guy. He was hired by the supervisor. Oh, and I heard he's probably traveling with a tan-colored German Shepherd who wears a bandana around its neck instead of a collar. Yeah, that's right; a bandana instead of a collar. Well, I appreciate that. You're damn right I'll press charges. He stole my pickup and ran off with two hundred dollars. When I get my hands on that damn long-haired hippy, I'm going make him regret he ever messed with me. No one steals from Big Jim and gets away with it! No one! Nah, I ain't gonna do something stupid. Just teach him a lesson. Well, again, I appreciate that. Thank you, officer, and get back with me as soon as you pick him up. Yes, sir, thank you. Oh, and you can expect a little something extra for the policeman's benefit this winter. Nah, no big deal. You guys earned it."

Hanging up the phone, Big Jim looked perturbed as he stared across his desk at the young man sitting quietly and patiently holding an envelope in his hand.

Controlling his anger, Jim said a bit more calmly to the visitor,

"Had an employee, that is a *former* employee, run off with a company truck and company money. But that's none of your concern unless you're looking for work," Jim said, leaning forward with a smile, "and I got an opening, Sport. Or is there something else I can help you with?"

"Yeah, if you'll have somebody unload the glass in the back of your pickup, I'd like to go home and get some rest." Reaching out across the desk and offering Jim the envelope, "and here's the money I didn't spend and all the receipts. I ain't showered in three days, and I think I'm startin' to get ripe," he said with a smile as he put on his yellow-tinted glasses and stroked the long blonde ponytail on the back of his head.

Big Jim's mouth dropped open as he looked the young man over, initially ignoring the envelope. He stood up, with both hands on the desk, and asked in a slow and menacing tone, "Just who the hell are you?"

Leaning forward from the chair, still shaking the envelope at Big Jim, the young man began, "Name's MJ. You sent me to Kentucky three days ago to get a load of glass for the factory. I drove straight through without stoppin' except for gas and to pee. Just slept in the truck to save money on a hotel, and I ate drive-thru. Figured you needed that glass in a hurry, and I like drivin' straight through. Saves time and saves money," MJ said as he shook the envelope again, offering it to Big Jim. "Now, would you mind gettin' someone to unload that glass; I am really burnt, and this here's what money that's left."

Taking the envelope with his left hand, Big Jim, with his mouth still agape, slowly smiled and even slower stuck his right hand out, "MJ is it, well it's mighty fine to finally meet you. Look's like I might owe you an apology there, young man."

Standing up to shake the man's hand, MJ said sarcastically,

"Yeah, it sounded like that a moment ago. You mind callin' the cops back so's I don't get busted headin' home."

Sitting down and continuing to smile, Big Jim said, "I'll do that. I'll do that right away." And as he picked up the phone and dialed, he took the remaining cash out of the envelope and handed it to MJ.

"Here's a little something for getting back so quickly, and I'll get that glass unloaded pronto. Let me just—Oh, hey, this is Big Jim again. I need to cancel that arrest on my employee that I said stole my truck. Haha, you're not going to believe this, but it appears it's all been a big misunderstanding. Yeah, you see, I kinda, well it looks like I kinda jumped the gun. But it's all straightened out now, so just go ahead and call off your dogs, haha. Yeah, I know. Sure, whatever you gotta do, just do it and send me the bill. Well, just do it!"

Walking outside, MJ hollered at the pickup truck, "Emmylou, come on and sit here with me in the shade while they get that glass unloaded."

Hearing her name, a big blonde Shepherd with a green paisley bandana tied around her neck jumped out of the pickup window and came running over to sit with MJ on the bench outside the office door.

Rubbing the dog's head and ears, MJ leaned down close to her ear and spoke, "Looks like folks around here judge ya without gettin' to know ya first. They sometimes say good things about you, but I don't think they really mean it." Then nodding his head back toward the office door, he continued, "You know what them fools thought we went and done. They thought you and me stole their truck and took their damn money. Why is it I gotta prove myself to folks over and over? Can't people just trust a man when they give him a job to do that he'll do it?" Leaning down to let the dog lick his face, MJ went on, "Maybe it's time we went back home. Whata ya say, girl. Wanta go back home to Florida? Shit, I'm beginnin' to wonder if we really belong out here, and here I went and bought them damn overalls."

Stepping outside, Big Jim approached MJ cautiously, keeping a watchful eye on the German Shepherd, and asked, "Say, there's just one thing I'm curious about. I called the glass factory's main gate late yesterday afternoon to make sure you got there alright, and they said you hadn't come through. Now, can you explain to me why that is?"

Looking up, MJ said with a bit of exasperation in his voice, "Like I told you, I drove straight through, so I got to the glass factory real early yesterday morning. The guard on duty checked me in and out. I heard him say his shift was over, and he was headed home to bed as soon as he got me loaded. You must of called the other guard that took his place, and of course, that guard never did lay eyes on me. I never figured you'd be checkin' in on me," and then after a pause and with a bit of disgust in his voice, MJ looked toward the forklift driver and said, "or I'd a left word at the gate."

Shaking his finger at MJ, Big Jim said, "You know it's things like that, imagination, that young people lack today. Yes, sir, imagination! Most folks wouldn't think about helping out the company; they just think about themselves. It's that kind of thinking that's going to get you places with this company."

Then directing his attention to the forklift driver unloading the pickup, Big Jim hollered, "Y'all be careful with that there glass. This fella here," looking back at MJ, "this one here with all that imagination drove all the way to Kentucky and back to get it, and I'm sure he don't want to turn around and go after some more just 'cause you in a hurry to unload. Now, be careful, I said!"

Walking toward the forklift, MJ could hear Big Jim saying as he shook his head from side to side, "Imagination! That's what these damn kids need nowadays. Imagination!"

Stepping out of the shower, MJ reached for a towel while he looked into the kitchen at his weary companion, Emmylou. After gulping down her food, she curled up on the blue-green vinyl-covered couch in the alley-like kitchen. Having a couch in the kitchen wasn't the ideal, but MJ shared the apartment with a friend named Carl. You see, the living room doubled as a bedroom for both, and it was so small there was not room for the courtin' couch. In the kitchen, the couch was against one wall, opposite the shelves that held a six-month supply of dehydrated backpacking food and various assorted pots and pans, including the meticulously seasoned iron skillet that Carl would not allow anyone to wash. Carl said soap and water would erase the many years of perfection in getting the skillet just right.

The backpacking food was a result of a trip planned for the Appalachian Trail. MJ and Carl had decided to hike the nearly twenty-two hundred-mile trail back at the beginning of the summer. They had prepacked the food, divided it into two-week rations, and sent it along with other supplies to various post offices along the trail. The plan was to hike for two weeks at a time, come off the trail for their post office deposits and then hike another two weeks. It was a grand plan, but MJ announced he had to make a detour out to Oklahoma for family matters and promised to meet up with Carl at Springer Mountain, Georgia, in time for the anticipated six-month hike.

But plans changed, and MJ ended up not making their rendezvous, so Carl began without him. Almost four hundred miles into the trip, Carl blew out his knee and had to be carried off the trail. He bought a Greyhound bus ticket and came to Oklahoma to rehab while living with MJ. They had all the post office drops forwarded to MJ's apartment.

MJ quickly wrapped the towel around him when he heard the front door open. Carl was surprised to find his half-naked roommate standing in the kitchen but not as surprised as the lovely young lady following Carl into the living/bedroom.

"I thought you wouldn't be back from Kentucky till tomorrow. Oh, this is Caty. Caty, this is my roommate, MJ."

Jumping back into the bathroom to throw on some jeans, MJ hollered, "I drove straight through. Just got back a couple of hours ago."

Stepping back out into the kitchen, MJ continued, "I'm just gonna' crash, so you two have the kitchen all to yourselves. You plannin' on rehydratin' some supper, or you goin' out? I made me some mushroom pasta alfredo earlier. Pretty damn tasty.The living room was divided by an eight by twelve battleship forty-eight-star American flag that at one time served as the couch cover and before that a bedspread, but when Carl moved in, it was repurposed again as a patriotic barrier to privacy. MJ picked up one corner and threw himself on his bed.

"Nice to meet you, Caty. Hope I see you in the morning."

And he was out.

The next morning Carl was up early rummaging in the kitchen, and MJ smiled, knowing that in some wonderful manner, the iron skillet would be employed.

"Hey, you need some coffee in there?" Carl shouted.

Stretching and yawning, MJ offered a refreshed, "That'd be great!" Then rolling out of bed and lifting the flag wall, he walked into the kitchen and rubbed Emmylou between the ears, who was reclining on the courtin' coach. Looking around, he asked, "Where's Caty? She already gone?"

"Yeah, she took off last night. Said she wasn't comfortable with you in the other room."

"Sorry, man. Seems like yesterday I surprised everyone. My boss wasn't expectin' me either."

"No big deal. Tonight I'm stayin' at her house. Her roommate went home for the weekend, so we got the apartment to ourselves," Carl said while handing a cup of coffee to MJ with a male smirk and a wink. "So, tell me about your trip. Anything exciting?"

"Well, the first day was uneventful, but we almost bought the farm later that night," MJ said, looking down at Emmylou.

"No shit! What the hell happened? You fall asleep drivin' straight through?"

"Nah, man. I hit a fog bank in the Kentucky mountains that was so thick that I couldn't see the hood ornament. So I decided to shut it down for the night and wait till it burned off. I eased the pickup off the highway on what I thought was the shoulder, but it wasn't no shoulder. Turns out, I had pulled off on the exit lane."

Easing a reluctant Emmylou over, MJ slumped down on the couch with his legs over the arm and set his coffee on the shelf across from the couch while continuing his recount of the trip.

"I had no longer got settled down in the seat after a couple of hits on a joint when there was someone knockin' at the driver's side window. I about shit my pants, man! There was blue and red flashin' lights comin' in from the back window and a big ol' cop standin' there a-knockin' with a big ol' flashlight. He motioned rollin' down the window with his other hand, and so I did without even thinkin' about the joint in the ashtray.

"You got truck troubles?" he said while sniffing the air of the cab.

"No, sir," MJ replied shakingly, "I couldn't see in this fog, so I thought I'd just pull over and wait till it lifted. Figured it would be a good time to get some shut-eye."

"You're right about this Appalachian fog. It's a bitch to drive in," he said while looking up and out into what couldn't be seen. "Even the locals learn to distrust it. I'd a done the same as you, except I'd made sure I was completely off the road before I shut off the truck. I woulda also have left the running lights on."

Looking down out the window at the solid white stripe line on the asphalt, MJ looked up and noticed the officer's name tag said, Anderson. Feeling justified, he smiled, "Officer Anderson, I made sure I was off the road and on the shoulder."

Hesitating and again looking off into the unknown, then back down at MJ with a seriousness that demanded the inexperienced out-of-towner pay attention, "Yeah, you was thinking right; however, this here ain't no shoulder. This here is an exit ramp," he said while waving his flashlight beam up and down the fog covered asphalt.

Letting this new and very important piece of information sink in slowly, he finally continued, "I was just going home, and this here is my exit ramp. It's a good thing I was coming off slowly, or I'da smashed into you and probably killed us both. By the time the fog lifted, they'd be havin' a double funeral."

Again, hesitating and looking up as if thinking about what to do with this obviously stoned-from-the-smell-of-it, long hair, the tired officer finally said, "There was an accident here at this exit a while back. A young mother and her son were killed in a fog just like this. A semi was exiting, and never saw them. Ran right over them and killed them instantly." Looking down at MJ, he continued, "The young boy would have been about your age now."

Then regaining some of his professionalism, he nodded with his chin up the road, "Why don't you let me pull around you and lead you to a safe spot to rest until the fog lifts. Besides, you don't smell like you're in any shape to drive anymore tonight."

"You mean he just led you off the exit and didn't even give you a ticket or bust you or nuthin?" Carl said while pouring more coffee into MJ's cup.

"No, in fact, he led me to a roadside park where other people had pulled off. Once I got parked, he hit his lights and then drove off. Pretty weird, huh? I mean, he had me if he wanted. I know he smelled the dope. I guess some cops is just decent and figure it ain't worth the hassle."

"Yeah, I guess so, although that ain't been the majority of my experience."

"Well, you just ain't livin' right, I suspect," MJ smiled. "Hey, you feel like twistin' one up and headin' up to Turner Falls?"

Monday morning, MJ arrived early at the glass factory. He wanted to check in with his supervisor, Tom, and make sure he scored some points for bringing the glass back so quickly. Maybe they would think of him when they needed more glass in a hurry. Emmylou had been allowed to come into the factory as long as she didn't bother anyone. She walked over to her usual corner and laid down, waiting for MJ's lunch hour. She didn't seem to mind the occasional scratch on the head or a partial sandwich thrown her way.

The supervisor, Tom, was an easy-going long-haired, bearded man several years older than MJ. In the summer, he wore cut-off blue jean shorts and handmade sandals made from leather and old tire retreads. In the winter, he wore the jeans before they became the shorts. MJ had heard that he had lived a while in Africa helping the locals dig wells for drinking water. MJ asked, "Peace Corps?" and Tom just smiled and said, "Nah, I'm just good with a shovel."

Tom was always fair, and in fact, he was the one that gave MJ and his previous roommate, Alex, their start here at the glass factory. The factory back then was in an old barn but was now located in an abandoned dairy facility. The large storerooms were naturally cool because of the thick concrete and heavy steel doors between rooms that never seemed to be closed even to the outside. This made the environment comfortable with all the many machines and handmade devices used for melting glass and reshaping it into glass swans for the carnivals and county fairs that relied on trinkets for the locals interested in taking an unusual memento home for the misses or granny's collection of odd glassware stored in dusty cupboards or on top of the TV.

"So, how'd the trip go. Quick, I heard," Tom said with an approving smile. "Seems like you made an impression on Big Jim. He said he wants to see you first thing when you got here. I think he's got a promotion in mind. I told him you would make a good supervisor."

"Supervisor! Damn, that's your job! I ain't takin' your job, Tom."

"Don't worry, he's talking about putting on another shift for some new orders coming in. I told him we sure could use the help. Go talk to him. I think there's a raise in it."

Before the day was through, MJ found himself promoted and, with a raise, the new night-shift supervisor. Big Jim sent him home and told him to come back the next night, and his crew would be waiting for him.

"Name's Adam, but folks around here call me, Dillo, you know, like an armadillo."

"Dillo? Why's that?" asked MJ.

"Well, I guess it's 'cause I been run over four times now. Last one that ran me over backed up and run me over again, but I only count that as one time," he said with a mischievous and crooked smile.

"But don't you worry about it none. I can still do my job despite the blackouts. Long as I don't pass out and fall into one of them flames," Dillo said with a laugh pointing at the many individual tables with gas flames coming out of hand-shaped metal tubes used to heat the glass to bendable temperatures. "Hell, if that happens, just have someone extinguish me and put me in the corner until my shift is over," giving MJ a wink, and with his smirk, Dillo leaned in and said, "I'm hard to kill. Just give me a try there, boss man." Dillo became the new tails and beaks man. It was the smallest flame used in the factory.

"MJ," Tom said, calling him over as he clocked in for the evening shift. "Afraid I got some bad news. Dillo tried to kill himself last night. He took a shotgun to his belly. He's in critical condition at the hospital."

Standing there with his mouth agape, MJ shook his head in disbelief and said, "He was fine last night. I think he was a little stoned, but otherwise, he didn't seem out of the ordinary. Do you know what happened?"

"Yeah, it seems he got in a fight with his girlfriend. Supposedly she was breaking up with him, and he couldn't take it, so he got real high and shot himself. I heard he isn't gonna make it. Do you want to go over to the hospital with me right now? I can get Claude to cover for you. I think it would be a good thing to do."

"Man, I ain't never done anything like this before. I don't know if I can handle it." Letting out his breath that he seemed to be holding forever, MJ said, "Let's go."

"And who are you?" the young intern asked while looking at the list of names on his clipboard.

"We work with Dillo—I mean Adam. I'm Tom, and this here is MJ, Adam's supervisor. We just wanted to check and see how he's doing."

Looking up and down the hallway and over his shoulder, the intern said with a lowered voice, "Normally, we don't give out information to anyone but immediate family, but I'm sorry to tell you Adam died about an hour ago. We are just waiting for his family to arrive and tell us their wishes. Again, I'm sorry to have to tell you this. Now, if you'll excuse me, I have another patient to see."

"MJ, I need you to go and represent the company at the funeral for…what was that kid's name?" Big Jim said matter-of-factly. His lack of emotion bothered MJ.

"His name was Adam, but we all called him Dillo. Sir, couldn't Tom do this? I ain't never been to a funeral before, and I don't really know how to handle it."

Looking up, Big Jim remarked in a surprising tone, "You've never been to a funeral! Haven't you ever had a close family member die?"

"Yeah, but I never went to their funerals. My folks just kept all that from me. I just think that Tom would be the better choice for the company."

"I got other things for Tom. You own a jacket and a tie?"

"No, sir, but I got some overalls."

After some instructions from Tom on the proper ways to conduct oneself at a funeral, MJ found himself sitting in the pew with the many people who came to pay their last respects to Dillo. His thoughts began to wander as he looked around and observed the various emotions people displayed. He wondered about the greater mysteries of life and death. He wondered why this much respect was not given in life. He wondered about all the various emotions he observed. Were they honest or just brought here to the funeral for show? He wondered if Dillo's former girlfriend was truly heartbroken or was her grief because everyone blamed her for this day. He wondered if the nice things being said really represented Dillo or could the truth not be spoken because we were in church? He wondered if God was really pleased to have Dillo or was He pissed over Dillo's decision to arrive unannounced. He remembered that if not for the alertness of a Kentucky highway patrol officer, this could be a service for him. He wondered what would people say about him? Would they lie to lessen their grief, or would they tell the truth and give the preacher more material to suggest another path for life? MJ looked to his right and then to his left and wondered if anyone would notice his tie was really his dog's bandanna.

At the instructions of the preacher, everyone stood and proceeded down the aisle towards Dillo's coffin. MJ thought it would be more efficient to just turn and exit out the back, but everyone seemed like they had done this before, so he followed their lead. The line seemed to bottleneck around the coffin, and MJ peered around the line and looking ahead, he saw Carl's new girlfriend, Caty, with her arm around Dillo's former girlfriend. He thought about jumping the line so he could be with someone who knew what they were doing when he saw the reason for the bottleneck. The coffin was opened, and people were leaning in and kissing Dillo!

"THEY'RE KISSING A DEAD MAN! A DEAD MAN!!"

MJ was startled by the volume of the voice that seemed to come from everywhere. He looked around to see if he could locate who was doing all the screaming, and at the same time, he noticed Caty was coming quickly to him with deep concern on her face. Several ushers from the funeral home were also approaching him rapidly. The shouting was getting louder when the ushers and Caty got to him. The ushers had forcefully reached in and taken MJ under the arms and were attempting to escort him from the line. Caty was holding his hand and whispering something to him like, "It's ok. It's ok. Let's just go outside. MJ, look at me. It's gonna be ok."

And then MJ realized all the shouting and protest was coming from him. He was the one upsetting everyone. He was the one the ushers were strong-arming toward the exit. He turned and looked over his shoulder back at the coffin and saw Dillo's mother just as she fainted next to her son. The preacher looked unsure how to salvage his message of hope amongst all this truth.

"He really freaked out? He was shouting at the funeral and everything?" Carl asked Caty while they stood in the kitchen.

MJ was lying over the arm of the courtin' couch, staring up at the ceiling while Emmylou tried to offer comfort to her distraught human by licking him on the cheek.

With regret in his voice, MJ said, "I told them I had never been to a funeral. I really didn't know they were gonna show Dillo's dead body. I don't even know why they would want to. Why would you want your last memory of a loved one to be lying in a casket with make-up on and a suit they never wore?"

With another moan, MJ raised himself up and sat on the arm of the couch facing Carl and Caty. He shook his head from side to side with his lips pursed together, staring at the linoleum floor. Then looking up into their faces, he said, "Promise me somethin', guys. If you're around when it's my time to go, don't let them put me on display. Just have them burn me up and dump the ashes. And for goodness sake, don't go and get some preacher to stand before everyone and tell them stuff just to make them feel better now that I ain't around no more. Hell, I guarantee ya' there ain't no preacher that knows me anyways. Emmylou knows me better than anyone; let her say somethin'. She'll tell the truth." Reaching behind, MJ scratched the dog between the ears and repeated, "You'd tell the truth, wouldn't ya', girl?"

Two weeks later, MJ and Emmylou found themselves driving the white Chevy pickup back through Kentucky. Reaching to adjust the static from the AM radio, MJ said to the dog, "Sure glad there ain't no fog this trip."

Just then, the radio cleared, and the newscaster continued with the local news,

This just in, apparently a twenty-year veteran of the Kentucky State Police, a Sergeant Walt Anderson, shot and killed himself in

his trailer this morning after working his evening shift. His captain told this reporter that Walt was a good and decent man. He said, and I quote, "Walt Anderson never abused his authority and never once did I have a complaint about the man." He went on to say, "he just was never the same after an accident killed his wife and son on Interstate 65." And now for the weather, it looks like it's going to be a clear night with temperatures in the...

VII

The Glass Factory Menagerie

*Memory takes a lot of poetic license. It omits some details;
others are exaggerated, according to the emotional value of the articles it touches...*
— Tennessee Williams, <u>The Glass Menagerie</u>

"I'm sorry, but we just ain't hirin' today."

"But your sign out front says you are."

"Well, that's an old sign I just forgot to take down. Maybe you should try over at the Sonic. I hear they hire college kids all the time."

"I don't go to college. I'm just looking for work that pays more than minimum. Damn! I'm a good hire. I work hard, and I'm honest. Why don't you give a fella a chance?"

"Now there ain't no cause to go and use profanity. This is a public place of business, we're church goin' people here, and we don't tolerate that kinda language in public. Why don't you take your attitude outside and be on your way? And put a shirt on! This ain't the river!"

I started to turn around and flip the manager off but thought better of it when I realized it would only add to his assessment of me, that I was "profane" in public. Besides, I needed a job, but I didn't need this guy spreading the word about not hiring the new longhair in town. I had no intention of cutting my hair for no job, and I damn sure wasn't buyin' no wig like my roommate, Alex. I could be persuaded to put a shirt on, but I had my limits. I just didn't understand why, in a state where the native Americans got away with long hair in the workplace, why couldn't an ol' beach bum let his *freak flag fly*.

"I'm tellin' ya, just buy a wig. That'll solve everything."

"But it's the principle of the thing. Why can't people just lighten up? I work every bit as hard as a short hair; in fact, I probably work harder. And besides, a wig would make me look ridiculous."

"So you're sayin' I look ridiculous?"

"Nah, man. What…what I'm sayin' is *I* would look ridiculous. You look great. No one can hardly tell that ain't your real hair. Seriously!"

"Bullshit! I know the wig looks like crap. In fact, I purposefully bought one that looked stupid to make a point. If folks around here are freaked out over someone's long hair and not a stupid wig, then the problem is in them and not what a person looks like. If people can't see someone for who they are, then they're the ones who got a problem, not me. You see, the way I see it is, it's society that's in need of a change, again, not me. It's like if you don't like Chevys, then don't buy a Chevy. But you don't have to go around and tell everyone that Chevys ain't no good cause maybe they don't care. Folks like Chevys, and you shouldn't make them think there's something wrong with a Chevy just cause you don't like something. You see what I'm sayin'?"

I had to admit to myself that I was not following Alex's logic, but maybe it was faulty because of the joint we were sharing and not his way of explaining the world around us. Maybe he was right. Maybe we shouldn't try to get everyone on our page and just let folks decide for themselves.

Anyhow, I broke down and decided to buy a wig. But buying a long blonde-haired wig didn't get me a job, so I cut my hair.

Cutting my hair was a big move in my life. For as long as I can remember, I have been looking for something that identifies me from the crowd. I believed that assimilating was not a path for me. I wanted—I *needed*—my own identity. I came by my insecurities the hard way by being bullied relentlessly all the way through junior high school. I hardly ever smiled. My hair elevated my status in a crowd to the level of *man ain't he cool!* The bullying stopped. It's as if my hair made me Samson. Not Samson in the physical sense, but Samson in the sense of my self-identity. I saw myself differently. I was no longer a wimpy kid who couldn't stand up for himself, but now I was someone who blazed his own trail. The world was what I made it, not what others defined for me. Now along comes these Delilah rednecks who want to tell me how to view life. They want me to go backward, and that ain't for me. But just like Samson, my hair got cut. And also, like Samson, it grew back, and I began taking down the temples of society—one at a time, as I saw fit, not as society designed.

Then I met a group of folks like me that railed against their own temples. Some succeeded, some failed.

"Hey, a friend of mine in class told me of this place that's hiring. You interested in going this afternoon?" Alex offered as I came in from a half-hearted attempt to find work.

"Yeah, let's do it."

"Ok, we'll take the '65 Dent. Let me get my wig."

Driving out of town west on Lake Road, Alex asked, "Where did you go today? Any prospects?"

"I went to that ice cream truck business to see if they had any openings. I drove one back home, and I thought maybe that would give me an edge."

"I didn't know that you used to drive an ice cream truck."

"Well, it wasn't for very long. In fact, it only lasted a day, or more like an afternoon, but yeah, I did."

"An afternoon? I got to hear this story."

"Well, long before I came here, I had gone home to see my folks. They had moved to a small town outside of Jacksonville. I decided I was going to stay for a while, so I looked at the Want Ads, and there was this ad that said they was hirin' drivers for ice cream trucks. I thought, how hard can that be? And besides, I liked ice cream.

I got to the place. It was in this warehouse district, and this dude at the front desk didn't even bother to check out my work history. He just asked for my driver's license, made a copy of it, and pointed to a truck back in the warehouse. It was an old Good Humor truck that had seen its day with "Dairy Treats" spray-painted over the original sign. It had a big mega-horn mounted on top for the ice cream music to play through. Then there was this other dude who loaded up the truck with all kinds of ice cream. You know shit like single-serve cups, DeLuxe bars, and Banana Fudge Pops."

"Ohhh! Did they have those Strawberry Shortcake bars? Man, I used to love those! And those…those uh, Orange Creamsicle Push-Ups! Man, they were my absolute favorite!"

"Yeah, they had it all. Now that dude that took my license, he didn't give me any ideas how to sell ice cream, he just told me the area I could sell in and not to cross the line 'cause I'd be in someone else's territory. He mentioned something about truck wars, but I didn't listen to what he was sayin'. Then he just told me to come back to the warehouse when I had sold the lot, and we'd settle up. Now the other dude that loaded up my truck, he was cool. We snuck around back to the alley and burned one, and he told me he gave me the truck that had an 8-track player in case I wanted to bring along my own music. Then he gave me some stupid-lookin' paper hat that he told me I had to wear while in the truck. So I grabbed some tapes and headed out to the area on the map they gave me wearin' that stupid-lookin' paper hat with the Dairy Treats logo in red on it.

Now I was pretty buzzed drivin' up and down the streets in those neighborhoods with that stupid ice cream truck song playin', wearin' that stupid hat and wonderin' where all the stupid kids were. Then I figured it out. They was all still in school. It was like one in the afternoon, and the kids hadn't got home yet. So I pulled over on this dead-end road and lit another joint. And then it came to me. If the kids were still in school, it stands to reason they'd be wantin' some ice cream when they got out. And so I drove around until I found an elementary school and parked right out front. I didn't think about how creepy it was that there was this stoned longhair sittin' in an ice cream truck out front of an elementary school. I was super buzzed, so I put in a Cream tape. You dig it, man? A Cream tape! Anyhow, I cranked it up and was just layin' back when I got the munchies and with all that ice cream, well, you know.

I was chompin' on a Nutty Buddy Cone when I heard this kid's voice on the tape askin' for ice cream. I finally figured it out that it wasn't on the tape, but it was some kid standin' outside yelling over the music. You see, I didn't realize the music was piped out through that big mega-horn on the roof. Turning the music down, I heard the kid ask how much for an ice cream. I told him it was sixty-five cents for a Nutty Buddy and fifty cents for a single-serve cup.

'I ain't got no money, mister,' the kid said, workin' up some tears. 'Some bullies stole my lunch money, and I ain't had nuthin' to eat all day.' Then finally turning on the waterworks full time and sniffing too, he looked up at me with a big PLEASE on his lips.

What could I do? I was too stoned to turn him down. So, I gave him a chocolate single-serve cup with a wooden spoon and told him to tell his friends. I figured that would get me some business.

It did. However, that kid must have told everyone that the longhair was givin' away ice cream. They all lined up, and they all put on their best story, and I gave away all the ice cream that damn truck had.

When I got back to the warehouse, it hadn't dawned on me that I was responsible for all that inventory. That's when I found out how the ice cream truck business works. After I paid the dude, he fired me."

Laughing, Alex managed to say, "You got fired! Fired in one afternoon! Man, that's got to be some kinda' record for ice cream truck salesman."

"Well, it turns out that it is remembered in that area. The cops got a warrant out for me for pushin' ice cream to little kids out front of an elementary school. Seems a mother phoned in about some suspicious character in a paper hat. I burned the hat."

Pointing suddenly to the left, Alex said, "Here's the turn-off, according to that sign."

"Man, you sure? There ain't nothing out here but an ol' barn."

"My friend said it was in an old barn. Hey, reach back there and hand me my wig."

We parked with the other cars up next to a barbwire fence. A lone bull looked up from his grazing and, not seeing anything of interest to a bull, continued his grazing. We made our way to the only single door beside the two large barn doors. Stepping in, I was struck by how dark it was except for the individual glows of single flames coming from various tables stationed around the inside. I was surprised the floor was dirt. Probably the original dirt from when the cows called this home. It certainly smelled like it. The barn was one big room except for the wall that still had the original stalls. I guessed for milking. The stalls appeared to be used for inventory of raw materials and finished products, waiting for packaging and loading onto trucks for shipping. No one looked up as we entered. It seemed there was an air of concentration at each station working with flame and glass. As our eyes adjusted to the dark and random lights, a tall thin man with long dark hair and mustache-less Amish beard noticed us and approached. He was wearing cutoff blue-jean shorts, a colorful red African dashiki, and what appeared to be handmade sandals from rough cut leather and used tire tread soles. He introduced himself as Tom, the factory supervisor.

Alex laughed at me as he pulled his wig off and threw it on the ground.

"Welcome to the Glass Factory. You lookin' for work? Here let me show you around and introduce you to folks. We're an interesting lot. I'm sure you'll fit right in."

Teresa

You know they say that marrying your high school sweetheart and then raising a passel of kids is the dream of many midwestern girls, but I kinda figure that was for a time long gone by. At least, that's what I imagine Teresa thinks as well. Every guy at the glass factory agrees that Teresa is the most beautiful lady they have ever laid eyes on. I would agree, except her dark eyes always look so sad even without the dark liner around them. I heard she married Jeff because he got her pregnant the night of prom. She later confessed to me at a dinner party for the factory menagerie that Jeff drove straight to the motel and bypassed the dance altogether that night. She told me she loved to dance.

Jeff worked construction, and work seemed to be seasonal for part of the year. Teresa had another child and then another before she admitted to herself she never was really that in love with Jeff. They just had great sex, but great sex doesn't always mean a great marriage, she would later lament. Jeff drank more when he earned less. Teresa had to get creative with what meager income came their way when it came to rent, utilities, and groceries. She made sure her children were fed and clothed, but come Christmas, things were a bit lean under the tree. So she went to work at the glass factory. In the darkness, her tears didn't show. In the darkness, sometimes, she would dance.

Jeremy

Vietnam didn't care if you agreed or disagreed with the politics that gave us the conflict that took so many of America's young and scared. At least, that's what Jeremy would often recite as he pontificated on the nasty habit of killing and cooking rats while a prisoner of their war for three years. He often declared that he was proficient at killing rats from thirty yards with a bamboo blow gun and darts of sharpened wood and feathers. He occasionally demonstrated his brag there in the barn that we shared with the rats. He fashioned a 36-inch glass tube from stock along with homemade darts he brought from home. I must admit that his skill was impressive, but I doubt his lunch, which he would cook over the flame used for reshaping the glass into swans, was that nutritional. In fact, I often felt it contributed to Jeremy's fantasy world of conspiracy more than the crop he brought home from Nam.

Jimmy

You know, sometimes you can just imagine from observing folks that somewhere in their history, some first cousins must have got together after a family reunion, discovered romance, and tied the knot. You know, an Edgar and Virginia or Jerry Lee and Myra Gale kinda thing. You suspect it in their children. Jimmy was such a suspect.

To say that Jimmy was slow mentally was not a stretch, but he sure made up for it in his responsibilities at the Glass Factory. Jimmy was the factory gopher and janitor. Whatever you needed, you simply had to holler for Jimmy, and he would get it for you *posthaste*. And it never seemed to matter to Jimmy how heavy the need was because Jimmy could lift anything. His strength never knew its limits. I once watched him move a whole crate of glass tubes so that Jeremy could chase a rat that was running for its life. Jimmy loved to watch Jeremy on the hunt. He often referred to Jeremy as John Wayne. Jeremy didn't mind; he said Jimmy reminded him of this crazy dude in Nam that went postal over some powdered eggs at chow. He went screaming into the jungle, blaming the Commies as loud as he could yell that they were directly responsible for the decline in America's breakfast. He yelled that powdered eggs were the real reason America had to go to war. He added that the Commies probably were responsible for Tang as well, not the space program as everyone believed. Jeremy said the dude never came back out of the jungle.

Jimmy was genuinely a nice guy. Many said it was because he was simple-minded; I believe his niceness came from a mind that simply couldn't find a reason to hate. He just loved. He used to say he loved Tom because Tom gave him a job when no one else would. He said he loved Jeremy because Jeremy protected those that couldn't protect themselves. He said he loved Tina because she was the only one who thanked him for doing his job. He said she even kissed him once, but no one could verify the event. He said he loved that crazy MJ because he had the courage to wear them damned tourist shirts in public even when they were on fire. Jimmy just loved.

Jimmy was loving when he died. He was trying to help an elderly woman with her groceries in the parking lot of the A & P when her husband heard her demands that she could handle her own damn groceries and to leave her alone. The husband grabbed his rifle from his window rack and shot Jimmy dead in the A & P on a Sunday afternoon. Folks said his last words were,

"John Wayne."

Tom

Tom took to running the glass factory after returning to Oklahoma from a stint several summers working in west Africa as a volunteer digging wells in an area where a good water source was only found underground. He first learned of the need from a college recruitment program run by the Knights of Compassion, an international organization that found cheap labor from sympathetic college-aged students ashamed of their affluence. Tom said he didn't come from an affluent background; in fact, he said that his life in Colorado prior to moving to Oklahoma was in some ways "more poor" than many of the people he met in Ghana.

"I was always good with a shovel. After miles and miles of diggin' post holes and stringin' fence, you kinda get good at it."

Tom said he always enjoyed the smiles on the people's faces when the water would begin to seep into the well. He said it was worth more to him than any amount of money for compensation. He carried that philosophy of satisfaction into the supervising of the factory since he certainly didn't receive the compensation he was worth. If one's goal in life was to build a career for retirement, supervising a glass factory was not the path to take. Tom's approach to the simple life of honesty and good character certainly made an impact on me.

And heck, I like making my own sandals.

Joseph

Joseph said he was the grandson of the great Olympic athlete, Jim Thorpe. Joseph said that he was born into the Sac and Fox Nation. Joseph said he wished all you damn white boys would quit playin' Indian and leave the real Indians to their own madness. I thought he was referring to my long hair as my Indian pretense, but he later explained it was my brag about playin' Indian in the Boy Scouts Order of the Arrow. He said we would never understand, so stop pretending.

I did learn from Joseph something of value. He decided his purpose in my life was to teach me to speak Okie.

"You Florididiots sound funny. No one can understand what you are sayin'."

So the lessons began. A word a day was what he offered in exchange for one of my prized *tourist shirts* (Hawian shirt to you non-Florididiots).

"*Mallanouer*. The speed limit is fifty-five mallanouer on the freeway."

"*Fraidy hole*. Head to the fraidy hole a storm's a-comin'."

But the word I remember to this day is *farr*. In the construction of glass swans, it is a multiple staging of individual parts completed by a number of workers. For the body—the only part we actually blow into the heated glass—the glass tube rolls on metal wheels over a hot flame, and when heated sufficiently, the glassblower will snatch the ends of glass not in the flame and quickly blow a puff of air into the heated part which ends up looking like a bubble in the middle of a glass tube. The bubble is then quickly set on an asbestos pad to shape the base of the bubble so it will later stand. As soon as one bubble is blown and seated, then another is ready. A glassblower can easily do three bubbles before emptying the table and loading the machine for another three bubbles.

Now let me say this about the Glass Factory, the majority of the machines were developed by either Tom or someone that Tom assigned to come up with a more efficient way of manufacturing. Tom recognized that I had some talent in formatting the process, so he tasked me to come up with a higher yield at the bubble table. I decided to build a four bubble machine. No one had ever blown more than three bubbles at one time. I was going to change that. The bubble machines were located near the open doors because of the heat they generated. We had two bubble machines, one behind the other with the glass blowers back to back.

Joseph worked the other bubble machine. He said four

bubbles would only lead to trouble, and we should abandon the effort. I convinced him to help me with the project. He said I was an idiot.

Once the machine was assembled, it needed to be tested. Now when it comes to working, I usually dress in blue jean cutoffs and an open tourist shirt. Joseph was standing behind me in his usual place on his three bubble machine, and I began the four. It was during the third bubble that I heard in a calm voice from behind, "Your shirt's on farr."

Looking down at my open shirt, I noticed flames were crawling up the cotton material at a rather rapid rate. The shirt must have touched the hot glass since it was unbuttoned and swinging freely with my movements. I quickly seated the third bubble, grabbed my shirt, and tore it off, throwing it out the double doors; then, without missing a beat, grabbed the fourth bubble and blew and set. Then I ran over to my flaming shirt and stamped it out. A crowd had gathered behind me, and they all applauded, to which I graciously bowed. A voice in the crowd said,

"Told you there'd be trouble, you idiot."

Alex

Speaking of the machines we invented, Alex *accidentally* invented a method for cutting the glass on a spray vase one night after a lunch break to Sonic. A spray vase is a single tube standing straight on its own base. That base is made by wrapping the bottom half of the heated glass tube around an asbestos mold that creates a circle within a circle allowing it to stand on its own. It is left with a tail sticking out from the mold that is then cut with a score from a small triangle file and then tapped to break the straight part of the tail off. In the next step, a tail-and-beak worker will close up the end so that the vase can hold liquid. Later, when purchased, the vase is generally filled with colored water and a spray of artificial flowers is often stuck in the vase for decoration. The problem with this score-and-break technique is in the hands of an inexperienced glass worker; the vase is often scored incorrectly, the vase breaks unevenly, and the vase is discarded.

During an evening shift, Alex came back from Sonic with a Route 44 cherry limeade coke that he took sips from in between forming vases. I was heating the glass, and Alex was wrapping the base on the mold. Then he would score the glass and break the tail off. He would give the hot glass a moment to cool before administering the scratch with the file and then the tap. Grabbing his drink in between vases, the sweat from the ice in the cup near the hot flame accidentally dropped on the hot glass, and it cracked perfectly.

Surprised, Alex simply tapped the tail, and it broke cleanly.

This gave Alex an idea. Lifting his straw from the cup with his finger over one open end to restrain the liquid, he let one drop of coke fall precisely onto the hot glass, and he got the same results. A perfectly cut tail and no loss due to incorrect cuts. A new technique was developed that night. Not only was it faster, but the loss due to incorrect scoring and breaking was no longer a problem. Our yield went up immediately. Management was pleased, although they wouldn't allow drinks at the machines. So Alex set a container of water next to the machine and would dip his finger in, collecting the water drop for scoring and breaking.

Yes, sir, Alex was smart, alright. Soon after training another on his *drop and tap* technique (a name Alex coined), he quit and moved back to Texas to start a band with a friend from high school. I tracked him down several years later at a club called Murphy's. After reminiscing, I made a request for my favorite John Prine song, "Illegal Smile." Today the song is always included in the band's set whenever I am in the audience.

Oh, and by the way, Alex never wore that wig again.

Raymond

Now Alex was smart, but Raymond, well, Raymond was scary smart. And weird too. He was the kind of smart that when he told you something he had done, you immediately doubted it was possible. For example, Raymond once told us that he had been the road tech for a popular rock and roll band called Vince Vance and the Valiants. He said he would have to rebuild the keytar (a keyboard held by a strap around the neck like a guitar) after every show because the musician would do a Pete Townsend and smash it on stage for the finale. Like I said, most folks doubted Raymond's stories, but one day Alex and I went to see the band, and after the show, Alex went up and asked the keyboard player if he knew Raymond.

"Raymond! Hell, yeah, I know Raymond! Best road tech we ever had. He used to rebuild the keytar every night 'cause it kinda got smashed. The dude was smart. But he was weird, definitely weird."

Raymond was weird, I guess because he ate a lot of acid, mushrooms, and peyote. The boy liked his hallucinogenics. He said it gave him a more spiritual focus and kept him in tune with nature. Raymond would often disappear on the weekends to commune with nature. When he returned, he would tell us of conversations he had with the animals and trees and rocks and things. I remember one time when Raymond came back from a backpacking weekend at Heavner State Park in eastern Oklahoma—he said he went to commune with the Heavner Runestone—that he had met this amazing raccoon that led him to another runestone in a gorge on private property next to the park. Well, I loved backpacking, so Tom and I decided to investigate, and Raymond said he would be glad to go along with us and show us the way. He said he had promised the raccoon he would visit again, and this would be an excellent opportunity to do so.

We spent two days tramping around every gorge we could find to no avail. Then on our last day, we went in the opposite direction, and there it was, just like Raymond said. We took a Polaroid of the stone, which I still have to this day.

Yeah, Raymond was weird, but his stories all seem to be true. Except for that one about the raccoon. It turns out it was actually an opossum.

Tina

If one could have a flesh and blood shadow, then Teresa's shadow was Tina. They were best friends since Tina's dad moved the family to Oklahoma from Chicago and took a job at the mill. They both were in second grade together in Miss Greer's class and were together all the way through graduation. Tina was shorter and thinner than Teresa, so she could and often did stand behind Teresa, and no one noticed she was there. That suited Tina just fine. She liked not being noticed. Her shyness made her somewhat attractive. At least it did with Dillo, Tina's boyfriend. Tina loved Dillo until she didn't. But that's another story.

When Tina talked, she often talked about the days she was bullied by her siblings. They often teased her that she was adopted. She learned later from her grandmother that it was her siblings who were actually adopted. But it was too late; the shyness had already taken hold. Her shyness kept her from her senior prom. Her shyness led her to the alter many times but only as a bridesmaid, never the bride. When Teresa told Tina she got a job at the Glass Factory, Tina naturally applied as well. A body can't go without its shadow, she thought. It was there she met Dillo. He was crazy and loved to laugh. He saw only the good in life, and he often said that Tina was the greatest good. Tina loved everything about Dillo except the dope. She never talked about the drunken stepfather that invaded her room at night and held her hostage to his inebriated passions that were meant for her mother, or so she believed. Tina's dreams often took her to a world where everyone was a true reflection of who they were and not masked by some substance. When Dillo passed out face-first into the beaks and tails flame from too many downers, she knew the future was over for her and Dillo.

She would later regret her decision to leave. But that's another story.

The only evidence that this zoo actually existed is in a small polaroid snapshot that hangs pinned to my office wall. This made up the menagerie that I worked with every day. These are the people I am so proud to have known, each one with their own temple to bring down.

The photo is of a time we all went to Teresa's house for a fourth of July celebration. There's Teresa with her sadness and dark eyes and darker liner, and shadowing her is Tina. Dillo was already gone. There's Tom with his Amish beard proud of us all; Joseph with his persistent scowl; Jeremy looking all crazy-eyed with his arm around Jimmy; Alex holding up his Route 44 cup next to Raymond and lying there on the floor in front of everyone with cut-offs and a Vietnamese smoking jacket with dragons embroidered on the lapels and no shirt was me.

And I am smiling.

VIII

The Case of the Murder of a Salesman

Many great authors have written wonderful tales that sometimes leave the reader questioning some little mystery left unresolved. Writers such as Shirley Jackson, Guy de Maupassant, and Flannery O'Connor come to mind. Questions such as the real motivation behind the Lottery, or what really happened to Madame Forestier's necklace, and who could forget the prosthesis-stealing Bible salesman, Manley Pointer? Ever wonder what else Pointer was guilty of? Well, that's where I come in. When I'm not grading papers or teaching class, I solve mysteries. I am Woody Farley—Literary Detective.

It was a hot afternoon, and I was not getting any help from the fan in my office. The air from it could barely lift the paper streamer attached to the grill. I had just finished working on the case involving that Macomber dame and was thinking about a little liquid diversion before launching into a marathon session of reading student papers. A knock at my office door drew my attention away from that particular task and from the temptation to reach for the flask in my hollowed-out Webster's dictionary.

"Come in, door's open," I said, looking up.

His tan told me here was a man who obviously spent most of his time shirtless, outdoors. The hands were the hands of one who worked with them, and the weather-stained boots said he worked outside, maybe on a ranch. I didn't recognize him as one of my students, which meant he probably was not here to see Professor Farley.

I indicated with my finger the only chair without a pile of papers and said, "Have a seat. How can I help you?"

"Name's Biff Loman," he said in a low voice as he sat down in the chair. Looking at me with some reservation, he continued, "I was told that you look into things…things that might not be as easily solved as some might think."

"I do wear other hats," I said, pointing to the old brown Fedora hanging on the hat rack along with the wrinkled trenchcoat.

Almost whispering, he said, "My father was Willy Loman… and I think he was murdered."

"Murdered, you say?" This brought my crime radar up. Easing back in my chair and eyeballing him carefully, I asked, "Why don't you lay it out for me. What makes you think your old ma—uh, father was murdered?"

He watched me guardedly as he began, "The insurance company said that my dad deliberately ran his car off the bridge and committed suicide. They said they had evidence that he had tried to do that several times before. Even said they had some lady as a witness. But I got to the car first, right after—"

he paused and swallowed hard before continuing, "—right after the accident, and I noticed that the skid marks stopped in the middle of the road. They did not swerve quickly like someone who decided to run deliberately off the bridge. I think he stopped in the road maybe to avoid hitting someone or something. My guess is that then someone hit my dad with something on the side of the head and pushed the car off the bridge."

He paused, looking down into his lap as he worked up the courage to finish his story

"When I got to my dad, I noticed there was blood on his forehead from smashing into the steering wheel, but I also noticed there was blood on the left side of his head as if someone had hit him with something."

"You know, when you're involved in a car accident, your body bounces around a lot. The side of his head could have smashed into the driver's side window." I was watching his reaction to this possible explanation and observed from his expression—or the lack of one—that he had already had this played out for him.

"I know that, Detective Farley, but the window on the driver's side was rolled down when I got there. When I checked it later in the junkyard, the window was intact and did not have any blood on it."

"Maybe his head turned and hit the steering wheel first before turning again and smashing…" pausing, I noticed he seem to get a little agitated by my continuing to suggest there might be some natural explanation.

"I thought about all that," he said calmly as he regained his composure, "but the wound on the side of his head did not match the wound from the steering wheel on the front of his head. I told the insurance investigator about all this, but he seemed anxious to close the case as a simple suicide. The police weren't interested either; they just seemed to go along with the insurance company and dismissed me as some sort of crook trying to get money from a policy. They said I needed a motive and some proof before they went chasing after some fool idea such as murder."

Folding my hands together and placing my index fingers under my chin, I studied him carefully before asking, "Do you have a suspect in mind? Maybe someone who had reason to knock off your father?"

"Yes! I think it was Stanley Carmon, a waiter at Frank's Chop House. He knew my dad had money on him that night and even told me that dad tried to give him the money, but Stanley said he put the money back in my dad's coat pocket. Like I said, I was the first one to get to the accident scene, and I leaned him back away from the steering wheel and noticed his coat pocket was turned inside out and the money was missing. My dad's friend Charlie said he gave him a hundred and ten bucks that day."

Looking up at me, Biff said slowly, "You find the one who took the money, and you'll find the one who murdered my father."

The next day I gave my students a library assignment and headed to the south side of town to the address the folk at Frank's gave me for Carmon. Apartment 32. Biff Loman certainly had enough reason to suspect foul play, and I wanted to follow up on his suggestion of finding the money. Stanley Carmon was as good a place to begin as any.

The apartments on the south side were bad business. I reached for my Webley-Vickers under the seat as I parked. Just as I was about to get out, a Chevy pulled in next to me so close that I had to roll down my window to bust the driver's chops.

"Hey, jerk! You think you could pull in a little closer to make certain I can't get out on this side of my car!"

"What's eating you, meatball!" he yelled back as he weaved up the sidewalk and up the steps to his apartment. Fumbling with the key in the lock, he unlocked apartment 32.

I gave him a moment to forget me before I exited out the passenger's side and bounded up the steps to the apartment. Guess I didn't wait long enough because he yelled at me again through bloodshot eyes when he opened the door, "What da' hell you want!'

"Name's Farley. Wondered if I could ask you a few questions?" I was hoping his obvious bender would loosen his tongue. "You Stanley Carmon? The same Stanley Carmon that works at Frank's Chop House?"

"Yeah, that's me. What'd you want?"

"I'm investigating the possible murder of Willie Loman."

This sobered him up, and he tried to hide his surprise when he said, "I thought Mr. Loman killed hisself runnin' his car off a bridge."

"Yeah, well, there's some evidence that suggests it was not an accident."

Stepping back and letting me in, he fumbled with his words. "You say—you say there's evidence that Mr. Loman was knocked off and it weren't no accident? Did someone see who done it?" he asked this cautiously, trying not to sound too anxious.

First thing I noticed as I stepped in was all the green champagne bottles scattered around the place. Guess Stanley took advantage of the stock at the restaurant. Focusing on what he had asked, I used what Biff said to me earlier, "Yeah, it looks like some lady witnessed the whole thing."

Now I could tell this really bothered him. He was looking around as if to figure out his best escape route. Reaching into his pocket, I heard him fumbling with his car keys. Changing the subject a little, I wanted to see if I could get him to give me something to hang him on. "Nice car you got outside. How much you give for it?"

Without thinking and looking toward the kitchen door, he said, "Hundred and ten."

"You know that's interesting. That's just how much that was stolen off of Mr. Loman during the murder."

"Hey! You sayin' I got somethin' to do with Loman's murder? Let me tell you—Willie Loman was alright in my book. His son Hap and me we go way back. I been in this neighborhood all my life, and I ain't never pinched nobody EVER! You got that! Now you need to get the hell out and stop botherin' decent folks."

Taking me by the arm, he pushed me toward the door. I reached into my coat pocket and jerked out my rod. He quickly let go and backed off. "I'm just trying to get some answers to some questions. If you think of anything, give me a call," I said as I handed him my card.

"Private dick, huh!" Throwing my card out the door, he said with disgust, "Go on! Get out and don't come back!"

Well, I certainly hit a nerve, but I needed more to go on before I could implicate Stanley in a crime. Just paying for a car that cost the same as what was stolen is not proof enough. I needed the murder weapon. And I knew just who I should see next.

There's something about a dame and her perfume. It's like a calling card. You know who it is before you ever see her. Trixie was like that. Even before you saw her, you knew she was in the room or had recently been there. Trixie worked for the county coroner's office, and it was not that hard to get her to look the other way when you needed something on a confidential report. Just a bottle of perfume and a compliment will work fine.

"What's doin' Trix?"

"Woody Farley! Don't you Trix me you, you, you two-timin' flatfoot!"

"Trixie, is there something bothering you, dear?" I was thinking quickly about what I could have done that set her off like this.

"What's bothering me? WHAT'S BOTHERING ME? Are you going to stand there and act as if you don't remember standing me up two weeks ago Friday? I waited for over an hour, in the rain, outside the restaurant, in my best dress and you never showed and you never so much as bothered to call me to explain why! That's what's wrong!"

This is one of those times that a guy's got to lay a line on a dame, or he may never get back in with her, so I laid it on thick. "But Trixie, sweetheart, I did leave a note pinned to your apartment door. You know I'd never stand you up unless it was absolutely necessary. Maybe the wind blew it off," I was fumbling now, trying to get my bearings and give her something she could believe. "I was workin' a stakeout and couldn't get to a phone."

Her expression changed suddenly because I knew how much Trixie loved my being a private detective. It was more romantic to tell her gal pals she dated a gumshoe rather than a college professor.

Her posture softened as she shook her finger in my face, "Well, since you were on a stakeout, I guess I can forgive you, but next time you better call."

Whew! I got past that one. Told you she was not that hard. "Here's a peace offering," I said, smiling as I handed her perfume. "And I was wondering if you could do me a little favor?"

She squealed with delight and did not pay any attention to the fact that the date on the box was older than our relationship. Again, she's not that hard.

Looking up and batting those mascara laden-eyelashes, she cooed, "What do you need, hon?"

"You remember a case a while back about a guy that ran off a bridge, labeled it a suicide. Name was Willy Loman. What was the official cause?"

Standing and working her walk over to the file cabinet, Trixie turned her head and smiled at me, then turning back quickly located the report.

"Let's see—Willy Loman, yeah, here it is. Loman, the official cause was blunt force trauma to the head. Open and shut. Why? You think there's more to it than that?"

"Any pics of the head injuries? Especially the left side of the head."

"Yeah, here's a good one. Looks like a nasty blow. You can see where it crushed the skull. Says here, pieces of glass were taken out of the wound. Must've hit his head on the driver's side window."

Working from a hunch, and remembering what Biff said, I asked, "Does it say what color the glass was?"

"Color? No, nothing here about color. But I guess if you promise not to stand me up Friday night, I might let you look in the evidence box."

After making several promises not to be late for Friday night, even for a stakeout, I headed back to my car with some information that might give me the evidence I needed to blow this case wide open. Pieces of green glass were taken out of the left side of Loman's head. Green glass—the kind champagne bottles are made of. The kind of bottles I noticed at Stanley Carmon's apartment. The kind they serve at Frank's Chop House. As I pulled away, I noticed a Chevy tailing me.

Stanley could use a lesson or two about how to tail someone in a car, but right now, the lessons would have to wait. I figured I needed to get to a public place and to get there quick. So I headed to Frank's Chop House for a bottle of champagne. I wheeled into the parking lot and went in before Stanley could get his Chevy parked. I asked for a table near the door so's not to be pinned in. They were just poppin' the cork when Stanley located where I was sitting, so I raised my glass in his direction. He headed over, none too happy.

"Won't you join me, Mr. Carmon, or are you working this shift?"

Looking around the restaurant slowly, he finally decided to sit across from me and poured himself a glass from the green bottle. Before he could put the bottle back in the bucket, I pointed at it and said, "You know they found green glass shards in the wound that killed Willie Loman. Green glass just like what that champagne bottle is made of."

Stanley swallowed his drink hard and then leaned across the table close enough that I could hear as he whispered, "I didn't have nuthin' to do with Mr. Loman's death."

"Well, it's interesting, Stanley, that Mr. Loman was missing a hundred and ten dollars, and that happens to be the same amount you paid for your Chevy. It's also interesting that your apartment is filled with green champagne bottles, the same kind of bottle that was used to murder Mr. Loman. Guess all we need to clear this up is your whereabouts on the night of the accident. Oh, I forgot. I already asked the owner when I came in, and he said you took off early that night, soon after Mr. Loman left. Now how do you explain all that, Stanley?"

I guess all this was too much as he reached across the table to grab me. Fortunately, he had been drinking all day, and his reflexes were slower than mine. I came up from under the table with a fist to his chin and knocked him backward out of his chair. Before he could scramble to his feet, I pulled my rod a second time on him and suggested he remain where he was if he knew what was good for him. I then told everyone that the situation was under control and grabbed Stanley by the arm to help him to his feet, all the while keeping my heater pointed where he could see the advantage to doing as I said. I threw a fin on the table and, over my shoulder, apologized to the management and then forced Stanley into the kitchen.

"Now, you want to tell me where you were that night, or do I have to take you to the coppers?"

Seeing no escape, Stanley slowly began to spill his guts. "I did leave after Mr. Loman. I thought about the money, and it bothered me a little too much, I guess 'cause I'd been drinkin'. Mr. Loman was talkin' out loud and mumblin' about his life insurance and what it would do for his boys. I knew what he was plannin', and I snuck down the alley just outside of his house and heard him shoutin' at Biff and Hap. I knew the man had snapped, and so, I just figured everyone would believe that it was suicide. When he drove off, I followed and got ahead and stood in the road so's he'd see me and stop. He looked at me and told me what his plan was and said it was a first-rate plan, according to Ben. I don't know who this Ben guy was, but I didn't think too long about it. I just remember hittin' him upside the head with a champagne bottle and grabbin' the cash." Pausing for a moment to reflect on what he had just confessed, he added, "If I'd been sober, don't reckon I'd done what I done."

About that time, the cops showed up, and everything was explained to them before they took Stanley away. I headed back to the office to spend some time looking up words in my Webster's. Just as I was reaching to refill my glass, I heard someone outside my door. Thinking it was the janitor who often cleaned my office late at night so that he too could look up words, I said, "Come on in. The door's open."

It was Biff Loman. "I heard they arrested Stanley. Thanks, Detective Farley. I knew my dad wouldn't have killed himself. He was not that kind of man." Handing me an envelope, he thanked me again as he left.

I almost told Biff the truth that Stanley had told me, but decided to let him keep his father as someone he admired. Reaching for the flask and filling my glass, I grabbed the first essay in the pile and began to read.

IX

The Case of Bad Country People

It was one of those late afternoons when one has too many papers to grade and too much whiskey in their coffee cup. The essays all seem to fade into the same topic. Not sure if it is the assignment or the Four Roses Small Batch. Reaching for the dictionary flask in my bottom drawer, I was suddenly interrupted by the phone ringing. Before I could answer, the voice on the other end started, "Farley, this is Frank. You got a minute? I really need your help!"

Frank Smithers, Vice Provost of the University. Frank and I had worked at the university for over 17 years, and not once had he ever asked for my help. Even when he was assigning me to some useless committee work, he never asked, just told me to get it done. His voice sounded urgent, and the fact that he was actually asking made me respond with, "Sure, Frank. Whata' ya need?"

"Something's been stolen, and I need to get it back right away!" and lowering his voice to a whisper, he said, "And need I say this is a matter that requires complete discretion? Ok?"

"Sure, but you're gonna need to tell me what's goin' on. Are you in your office right now?"

"No, but I can be at yours in fifteen minutes. I'll fill you in then," he said as he hung up the phone.

Whatever it was, Frank was not the excitable type. It was out of character for him. As I was thinking about Frank's problem, a voice from the doorway, as silky as a rose petal, said, "Excuse me, Professor Farley. There's a student here to see you." The voice: departmental secretary, Audrey Finebody.

Audrey Finebody. She came to the university from somewhere back south. I'm not quite sure where and there seems to be a bit of a mystery surrounding her application and what it did not contain. Nevertheless, she was hired on the spot, probably due to the fact that Darius McQuery was on the committee, and everyone knows he has an eye for the ladies. I thought to myself that someday I'll have to look into that mystery. What I didn't know was how soon "someday" would come.

"Eh hmm," mumbled a student standing before my desk. I faked a preoccupation with a stack of papers, because I like to give the students the impression that a professor is busier than what he might be.

Looking up, I noticed how thin the student was and how desperately he needed a suit that fit him. He looked out of place—not the fact that he had a suit on—but the fact that he had one of those car salesman smiles, thinking it would get him somewhere with me. I also noticed he carried a big Bible under one arm and an old valise in the other.

Dropping the valise, he extended his hand without losing his smile and said, "Manley Pointer. How do you do, Professor Farley? A friend of mine recommended your class if ever I should find myself at this university. Now, I know the semester has begun, but I sure would appreciate an override, and I will do my darnedest to catch up with what I've missed. You see, I've been out of state all summer selling Bibles back south to make my tuition. In fact, I just sold a Bible to the Vice Provost,

Dr. Smithers, this very morning. Ain't that a coincidence?"

This kid sure had the gift of gab, but the real coincidence was the fact that in the last few minutes, Frank Smither's name came up twice. I wondered if Frank's urgency had something to do with this Pointer fellow. I decided to stall him and find out what I could until Frank arrived.

"It is rather late in the semester to be signing up for a class. Who did you say recommended you?"

"Joy Hopewell. I met her a while back when I was down in Georgia. We were on a picnic when she said that if ever I find myself at your wonderful university that I should look you up and take your course in Comparative Lit."

"Hmm, Joy Hopewell. I do not recall that name, but of course, I've had a lot of students over the years. When did she attend this college?" I noticed that when I pressed for some information, Pointer got a little nervous and dropped that car salesman smile.

Standing and grabbing his valise, Pointer said, "Listen, I just remembered I have to be across town in a few minutes. Do you mind if I come back later?"

Just then, Frank rushed into the office without stopping to announce himself to Miss Finebody. He drew up short when he realized I was with a student, but then his demeanor changed when he saw who it was.

"YOU!" Smithers yelled, shaking a finger at Pointer. "WHERE THE HELL IS MY EYE?"

It was at that moment that things got a little crazy. Finebody had rushed in to announce Smithers at the same time that Smithers had halted. They bumped into each other, which pushed Smithers into Pointer. Pointer was attempting to move around Smithers and head for the door when he got tripped up by his own valise. As Smithers grabbed for the back of Pointer's suit coat, Pointer was crawling toward the door and through the legs of Finebody, who seemed to be frozen to the spot with all the excitement. Finebody screamed as Pointer exited the office with his Bible and valise through her legs. Smithers, who was off-balance, fell into me as I came around the desk to help catch Pointer. Regaining his balance, Smithers turned to head out the door after Pointer as Finebody screamed again and jumped out of his way right into my arms. She hesitated against me and then stood back, smoothing her clothes. At the same time, Smithers ran down the hall, yelling, "Come back here, you lousy sonofabitch!"

"You ok, Miss Finebody?" I noticed she was blushing, and I wanted to think it was connected to the hesitation in my arms. It wouldn't be the first time some gorgeous doll fell for Woody Farley. She smiled and smoothed her dress as she turned back into her office. Smithers came back out of breath from the chase—without Pointer.

"That lousy S.O.B. got away! Farley, you got to do something. I gotta find that kid!"

"You haven't told me what's going on, Frank, and did I hear you right that that kid stole your eye?"

Reaching back to shut the door, Smithers sat down and pulled his handkerchief from his pocket to wipe the sweat from his forehead. Gathering himself and leaning back in the chair, he began, "I've had an artificial eye since the war, but I was too vain to let anyone know." Leaning forward, Smithers said with some reluctance, "I didn't tell anybody, not even you, but I'm getting married this Saturday, and I need that eye! My backup doesn't fit that well."

It was at that time I noticed that Frank's right eye was looking right at me, but his left was staring at the floor. It's probably not a good idea to have a roving eye at your wedding. It's pretty hard to convince your bride-to-be that you really mean I do when your eye is on the bridesmaid. For whatever reason, Smithers didn't want anyone to know about his upcoming nuptials, so I asked only about his encounter with Pointer. "Tell me what happened, Frank."

"Earlier this morning, I was in my office polishing my good eye for the wedding when this punk Pointer came in wanting to sell me a Bible. He started talking about my eye and asked if he could hold it. I thought he was a bit strange and put it away in my desk drawer while I went to get my checkbook. I almost stumbled over him as he was coming out of my office. He just took the check and ran off. I didn't realize 'til a little later that the eye was gone. That's when I called you."

Grabbing my Fedora and trench coat, I told Frank not to worry; I'd find his eye in time for his wedding. However, finding Manley Pointer wasn't as simple as I led myself to believe. I had gotten an address from the Registrar, but the landlord said that Pointer had left that morning and he hadn't seen him since. I played a hunch and decided to stake out the building from the alley.

Around three in the morning, my hunch paid off. Creeping quietly down the alley was Pointer. He stopped below a window and listened for a moment before crawling through. I decided to give him a moment to get settled when someone else came slipping down the alley. This second person was obviously a woman by the shape the alley light cast against the wall of the building. There was something familiar about this woman. Instead of crawling through like Pointer, this lady quietly tapped on the window. After a few moments, Pointer raised the window and spoke briefly, and from the muffled tones and body language of the woman, I could tell the conversation was more of an argument. As the woman turned to leave, the light from the alley lamp shone brightly on Finebody's face!

I decided to get to the bottom of Miss Finebody's appearance later, but for now, I needed to get Smithers' eye back. As I made for the window, I heard a shot from inside the apartment. Carefully climbing in, I landed in a dark room. There was a light on down the hall, and as I headed toward it, I fell over something lying in the middle of the floor. Picking myself up, I reached for a match to see what it was.

It was Smithers.

While getting back on my feet, I heard the front door slam. Fumbling for a light switch, I felt Smithers for a pulse. He had none. I didn't know how Smithers found Pointer, but it got him killed. I needed to catch up with Pointer and get some answers fast. Heading out the door, I stopped at the landlord's to let him know about the body in 2A, then I headed for my car. I circled the area twice but didn't find any sign of Pointer, so I headed back to his apartment to see if I could pick up any clues.

"Farley. Figured you was connected when the landlord fingered a man wearin' a Fedora and old trench coat. Whata' ya' know about the body here? Is this any of your handiwork?"

"Sergeant Burgess, nice to see you, too! And, no, this ain't my work, but I do know who he is. His name is Frank Smithers. He's the Vice Provost at the university, but that's all I got."

Just then, a rookie called from another room, "Hey Sarge, you better get in here. You gotta see this."

"Man was this guy some kinda' nut or what?!" exclaimed Burgess as he pushed his hat back on his head and looked with amazement at the assortment of artificial limbs shoved into the kitchen pantry. And on a shelf by itself was a polished glass eye.

I knew the rest of the night would be spent cataloging the fake limbs and such, so I headed on home to get some shuteye before class in a few hours. I also needed to see how Finebody was connected to this.

After class, I headed back to my office, but before I could question Finebody, she announced, "You have a visitor in your office. I think he's with the police."

"Burgess, what can I do for you this morning?"

"You can begin by telling me what you know about last night."

"I told you everything. I'm as clueless as you." I knew that by insulting him, he might give me what he had just to boast.

"Now cut the crap, Farley. I know that if you're hangin' around a crime scene, you gotta' be workin' a case. Now spill before I haul you in on suspicion!"

Well, insulting didn't work this time. Ok, I'll try the mutual sharing angle and see where it leads. "I was following a kid named Manley Pointer. He stole an artificial eye from Smithers, and I was trying to get it back. I saw him climbing in the window last night, and then I went in after him. That's when I found Smithers. I haven't been able to locate Pointer yet. That's all I got. What'd you get?" I conveniently left out Finebody's appearance 'til I had a chance to talk to her.

Taking out his notepad, Burgess began to write, "Manley Pointer, huh. How do you know this kid?"

"He came into my office yesterday to register late for a class. That's all I know about him at the moment. Now I've cooperated; how about you giving me something."

Burgess closed his notepad and left without a word. It was his M.O. sometimes to leave me hanging until he thought he had one up on me. I noticed Finebody had been listening from the outer office, so I called her in to see what part she played in all this.

"Miss Finebody, I saw you last night outside the window talking to Manley Pointer. What were you doing there, and how do you know this Pointer fellow?"

Finebody was not able to conceal her surprise, and she knew that I sensed it. She lowered her eyes and then spoke as if this burden was too much to carry any longer. "I went there last night to try and convince Manley to return the eye before it was too late."

"How did you know where this punk lived? Did you two meet before?"

Looking up at me, she said, "He's…he's my brother."

"Your brother!"

"Well, he's actually my half-brother. We have different fathers. I thought if I could get him to return the eye, we might avoid another embarrassment for our family." She then put her face in her hands and began to cry. After a moment, she regained her composure and continued. "Professor Farley, Manley's a good person. He just got caught up in this black market prosthesis racket. He owes money to some really bad people. A lot of money! They force him to steal to pay back what he owes. But Professor Farley, Manley didn't kill Dr. Smithers. Even with all his faults, Manley just isn't capable of killing anyone. I just don't believe he did it."

She lowered her head again and cried a little more. Now I've been suckered by a dame's tears before, but I really felt Finebody's were genuine. I had a hunch if I found the guys Pointer owed money to, I might then find who killed Smithers. "What can you tell me about the people Manley owed money to?"

Finebody said she didn't know who they were, but she told me where I could find Pointer, so I headed out to the local YMCA. With any luck, I could get some answers from Pointer before the cops got to him.

The guy at the front desk said he recognized Pointer as the kid in a badly fitting suit who tried to sell him a Bible, but he said that Pointer had left early that morning with some guys in a blue Ford. He also said that Pointer didn't appear to go willingly.

I knew that if I was going to find Pointer, I'd have to call on my snitch, Barry the Mouse. Barry didn't like the moniker that was laid on him by those on the streets. It seems he was always the uninvited guest at any back-alley dealings, and no one seemed to know who invited him. I found Barry hangin' out at his favorite beer joint, The Jug.

"As I live and breathe, if it ain't the good Professor Farley. Been a while since I seen you in this part of town. I suspect you ain't here because you like the brew. So, what can I do for you, Pro-fes-sor?"

"Know anything about a new gang in town stealin' artificial limbs and such?"

Changing his tone, Barry said, "You serious, Farley? You mean like wooden legs and hooks and stuff?"

"I think they've improved them since the pirate days, Barry."

Motioning me to the back of the bar so we would not be overheard, Barry said in low tones, "Yeah, I heard 'bout some weird stuff goin' down in town lately. Seems there's this weird guy and his crew from someplace back east buyin' and sellin' that stuff. Don't know why anyone would want that kinda' thing, but there must be a market somewhere, or maybe their leader got him a thing, you dig? I heard they's a pretty mean bunch, and you don't mess with them no-how. You be careful, you hear, Professor? They play for keeps."

Well, the Mouse came through, and he gave me an address. I circled the block a couple of times to see if there was any activity in the building before parking across the street. Checking to see if my rod was loaded, I headed for the door remembering Barry's advice. Just as I was turning the doorknob, it pushed open, and Manley Pointer came rushing out, still carrying that Bible. I slammed the door on an arm that was blasting away at Pointer at the same time I was shouting, "Head for my car, Pointer, and keep down!"

Pointer quickly leaped into the back seat as I was beatin' a path for the front. I managed to get a shot or two off, and that slowed those in the building, which gave me time to fire up the Lincoln and hit the gas. In my mirror, I saw at least three or four runnin' out, but before they could get any more shots off, we were out of range and soon long gone.

Once I felt we were in the clear, I pulled into an alley and parked. Turning to Pointer, I noticed he was visibly shaken. I get a little rattled too when someone is blastin' away at me.

"You ok, kid?"

"OK! Jeez, I just got shot at, and you want to know if I'm ok? No, I'm not ok!"

"Take it, easy, kid. Just breathe and then tell me what happened."

After a moment, he started in. "Last night, I don't know-how, they found where I was staying and were waiting for me. They had that guy Dr. Smithers. He was beat up real bad. I felt bad for the guy. I mean, he bought a Bible from me and told me he was gettin' married this weekend. And then they just shot him! After that, they brought me to that warehouse. I heard one of them say that Dr. Smithers had brought you onto the case and that it was getting too hot to stay. That's when I beat it for the door. And, well, you know the rest."

"Listen, Manley, I know that Audrey is your half-sister. Why didn't you just leave with her or send her for help?"

Looking at me surprised, he said, "Because I didn't want her to get involved with these guys. No telling what they'd have done to her." Then he began to break down and cry. Through his sobs, he managed, "I've done a lot of bad things, Professor Farley, and I've disappointed my family. I'm not about to get my sister killed because of what I've done. Can you help me, Professor?" He looked up at me pleadingly.

Like I said before, I can tell when someone is working me with their tears, and for a moment, I wanted to believe Pointer, but something was gnawing at me about what he had said. Something just wasn't adding up right. I knew I'd better use caution, or I might end up like Smithers.

I dropped Pointer off at a safe place and told him to lay low until I had something to work with. He wasn't too happy about me going off without him, but in the end, he agreed. I stopped off at the university to get some more details from Finebody on Pointer's past and then headed back to see Barry the Mouse. Barry told me something that he hadn't mentioned before, and it all came together. Now that I had the whole picture, I went back to pick up Pointer, but he was nowhere to be found. I figured it was time to bring Sergeant Burgess up to date because I might need his help. Then I headed back to the warehouse. Slipping in quietly through a back door, I overheard the goons talking about skipping town with all the heat on them now. One voice protested, however, saying that the town's right for picking and he could handle any heat that came his way. After all, he said, he'd taken care of Smithers, hadn't he? I drew my rod and stepped out and said, "Ok, everybody reach for it, and that includes you—Pointer!"

"Well, Professor, it seems I underestimated you and your talents. But I believe that you underestimated me and my crew. I don't think that one pistol will take care of all of us. Do you, Professor?" Pointer said with a smirk as his crew all drew their guns.

From behind them came another voice, "Maybe not one pistol, but how about a dozen or more?" Sergeant Burgess and his men came in just in the nick of time, and I must say I was none too proud to see them.

"How did you figure it out, Professor?" asked Pointer as an officer was putting on the handcuffs.

"Well, I had my suspicions when you said that Smithers told you about the wedding. You see, he hadn't told anyone, not even me. I guess your sister heard him from outside the office, and she told you that night in the alley. She also told me about what happened back home at the hospital where you worked and the trouble you got into in the prosthetic lab, and all the embarrassment it caused your family. You got one strange fetish Pointer. Oh, and one other thing, the word on the street was that the new crew in town was led by a guy who was into weird stuff and carried a Bible. Guess that about sums it up. Get him outta here, Sarge."

Later, while enjoying a slug from the dictionary flask, Finebody came into the office, and I offered her one. She took it and sat down across from the desk and let out a sigh.

"Well, I guess it's all over now with Manley finally in jail. I'll turn in my two weeks in the morning and head back home."

"Why do you want to leave? You were just settling into the routine here, and besides, who's gonna' accompany me to dinner this weekend? I said with a wink and a smile.

Looking up and smiling back, she stood and turned to leave the office. Hesitating, she looked back over her shoulder and said, "Maybe I will stick around. Oh, by the way, you got a package from someone named Snopes from New Orleans. It's marked 'Urgent.'"

X

Peeing on the Chairman of the Board's Shoes

"Man, I like what they've done with this place," Zeek said as he sipped from his Irish Mule of Jameson, ginger beer, and lime, and glanced around. "Can't remember the last time I was down here in Galveston."

"Yeah, you should've seen the Balinese in the fifties. Back in the days of Hope and Lee and Ellington. Man, this place was jumpin'. And when The Voice sang, mannn! Ol' Blue Eyes. Now there's a cat who could swing."

Always reflective, Dave raised his eyebrows as he looked quizzically at his friend Mickey.

"Which Lee? Tommy or Geddy?" asked Zeek.

"Peggy Lee," Mickey shot back as he raised his original Margarita and gestured toward both Zeek and Dave, the way he usually did when he was about to launch into one of his *did you know* stories.

"Did you know that right here in this very bar, the Margarita was invented? That's right. A fella by the name of—of uh, what was his name? He was a bartender, actually. What was his name? Oh yeah! Cruz, Santos Cruz in '48. He was tending bar, and Miss Peggy Lee—Miss Peggy *Margaret* Lee—was performing that night, and ol' Santos made her a drink on the spot, a brand new creation that he named after her." Then, lifting his glass reverently high, "The Margarita!"

Zeek looked at Dave, and Dave looked at Zeek. They both began to smirk, but Mickey continued:

"Ol' Santos. Yeah, he was all right. Did you know that he was the one that gave me my first drink of whiskey? My first drink—right here in this very place," he said as he tapped his finger on the table for emphasis. "Down at that end of that bar," he gestured, pointing to the bar. "Me and Frank Sinatra throwin' back drinks together and getting 'gassed' as Sinatra would put it."

Dave raised his eyebrows as Zeek choked on his drink. "You and who? Frank Sinatra! How many of them Margaritas have you had there, Mickey?" Zeek questioned as he leaned forward toward his friend, expecting to hear some back-pedaling explanation.

"When did you ever stand at a bar with Frank Sinatra?" Dave asked.

"Oh, it was a long time ago. I was pretty young when it happened. In fact, I guess I was only eight or so at the time. Don't remember exactly. It was back in the summer of fifty-seven when this place was shut down for gambling. Back when the brothers Maceo—Sam and Papa Rose—ran the joint. Sinatra was a regular, and I came in with my uncle, the Texas Ranger."

This time Zeek set his drink down before choking again in disbelief, "Your uncle was a Texas Ranger, yeah right! And my mother was the madam at La Grange."

Dave's eyes were stretched wide now as he looked at Zeek in wonderment, then nodded with a grin.

Mickey settled back into his chair and paid no attention to

either Zeek or Dave as he sipped his Margarita, and, slowly, a smile came across his face.

"Yeah, I had this uncle who worked for the Texas Rangers, and he would come here in the mid-fifties and sometimes just sit. He'd sit and watch for anything—anything that might help bring down the Maceo brothers. You see, the Rangers knew something was going on. But, the brothers were smart. The pier out there is six hundred feet long. They called it 'Ranger Run' because the Rangers would sprint down the pier trying to get to the gambling room before all the evidence was stashed away in a safe. The brothers had this system. When a Ranger was spotted running down the pier, they sounded a buzzer in the back room, and, in less than two minutes, the chips, cards, and slot machines were all out of sight. If the Rangers ever got there, all they would find were pool tables and bridge tables. I say 'if' because when that buzzer sounded, the band would strike up 'The Eyes of Texas.' All the patriotic Texans in the restaurant would stand up, making it even harder for the Rangers to get through the crowd to that back room.

Dave looked at Zeek, and Zeek looked at Dave. They both just smiled and nodded at Mickey as they settled in for another of Mickey's dubious tales.

"You see, this uncle of mine knew I liked Sinatra 'cause my mom had all his stuff. I would go around the house all the time just singing to his records. One day, my uncle dropped by on his way to the Balinese, and he up and asked if I'd like to go there to get something to eat. My mom, she didn't approve. She was all worried about the kind of people she had heard hung out there. But my uncle, he was cool and assured her that he would not let me out of his sight—even to go to the bathroom. And besides, he said, 'We might even run into Ol' Blue Eyes hisself.' Well, that did it. There was no way that I was going to miss this chance to see Sinatra.

"So my uncle and me, we headed to the Balinese. The head waiter recognized my uncle and set us up at a table that seemed to be reserved for folks like him. We had a perfect view of the place. I could see everyone who was there, and if Frank Sinatra walked by, I'd spot him.

"After about three cokes, I told my uncle I had to go to the bathroom. He pointed me in the direction I needed and seemed to forget all about his promise to my mom.

"Now, remember, I'm only about eight, and peeing in front of a stranger was a big deal for me at the time. Fortunately, the bathroom was empty when I went in, so I moved straight toward a urinal to do my business.

"Suddenly, the bathroom door opens behind me, and this guy walks in and sets himself up in the urinal right next to me. Well, I'm so self-conscious I don't even look up at his face. I mean—I'm freaking out. Here's this guy dressed in a suit. He walks in. Sets himself up and doesn't even leave an empty urinal between us. All I can think of is to get my business done and get out of there.

"'How ya doin' kid?' the man asks.

"I froze. Here I am, standing in front of the urinal, and this guy's talking to me. I look up at him, and there he is! The leader of the Rat Pack himself. Peeing right next to me! Frank Sinatra, the biggest name in show business, peeing like everyone else. Before I realized I was staring up at him, he sticks his hand out and says...

"'Hi, I'm Frank. What brings you to this clam-bake, kid?'

"I can't believe it. Not only does he want to talk to me, but he's actually wanting to shake my hand. At first, I lean away when

I think about where that hand has been, but then I remember what my father taught me about shaking a man's hand.

"Don't cha' ever refuse to shake a man's hand when he puts it out there for ya.' And for goodness sake, don't shake a man's hand like some wimpy, little snot-nose kid—you hear? Take his hand and give it a good strong wringing. Got that?'

"So I turn to take Sinatra's hand, but then I realize that I was still peeing as I turned, and I ended up peeing all over his shoes. My God! I'm peeing on the Chairman of the Board's shoes! Jeez! And then it hit me. I remembered that Sinatra was supposed to have Mafia connections. So, I began to cry as I thought about the possibility of some rather large dark-suited, sunglass-wearing men showing up at my door late one night asking for Mickey. I cried even harder as I pictured one of them reaching slowly into his jacket and removing a long, gleaming knife that could only have one purpose. They were going to make sure that I never peed on Sinatra's shoes again, or on anyone else's, for that matter.

"'Hey, kid! You're peeing on my shoes! You mind pointing that thing in another direction,' Sinatra yelled as he stepped back away from the urinal.

"I cried even harder.

"'Stop your fussing, kid. It ain't no big deal. I've done it myself after a few and gettin' gassed.'

"I stood there just looking up at my idol. I managed to quit peeing and was quite embarrassed that I had exposed myself to Mr. Sinatra. Thankfully, he didn't seem to pay any attention to it, and I thought this was just too marvelous for words. As he shook each shoe, he mumbled something about having to go on stage and perform, and this was certainly not a good thing to have happened right before a performance.

"I...I'm...I'm real sorry, Mr. Sinatra,' I said in between sobs.

"'Oh, don't mention it, kid. I'm a big-leaguer. There's been worse things that happen before goin' on stage. Say, you ain't told me your name, kid.'

"Mickey. Folks, just call me Mickey, sir. I mean Mr. Sinatra.

"'Well, Mr. Mickey, I think I need a drink, so I ain't so hacked about this situation. You wanna swing with me at the bar? I'm buyin'. Whata'ya say kid?'

"Man, the thought of me and Frank Sinatra sidling up to a bar and throwing back a few was too much for my ego. Just think what the other kids would say. Me. Mickey Delgalo tradin' shots with Frank Sinatra. Why I might even start my own Rat Pack. Heck, after a few drinks with Ol' Blue Eyes, he might even make me an official member of 'the' Rat Pack. Frank, Dino, Sammy, Peter, Joey, and Mickey. I could see it now the six of us pallin' around together, playin' pool, hustlin' the babes, doin' Vegas...

"'Yer old enough to swing, aren't you, kid?' Sinatra said with a wink.

"I hesitated as I tried to remember just what the legal drinking age was and just how many years before I would be legal.

"'Well, don't sweat it, kid. I'll order you a scotch and milk ya' dig. That'll get us by the coppers. Come on, what do ya say? You game?'

"A scotch and milk! A scotch and milllk! Think of what the kids would say, 'You traded drinks with Frank Sinatra at a bar, and you had a scotch and milllk!'

"Anyhow, when we came out of the bathroom, Sinatra asked where my folks were, and I told him I was there with my uncle. He suggested we ask him along. So, I got my uncle, and we hooked up with Sinatra at the bar.

"'Hey Santos, give me a bourbon and a scotch and milk for the kid here,' Sinatra told the bartender with a wink. 'And whatever this here Charley wants,' motioning to my uncle.

"This time winking at my uncle, Sinatra said to me, 'Come on, kid. Grab your drink, and let's go throw some dice in the back room.'

"So, that's just what we did. Me, my uncle, and Frank Sinatra throwin' dice and sippin' drinks in the back room of the Balinese with the Maceo brothers.

"It was about then that my uncle whispered to me and suggested I go to the bathroom. I guess he forgot that I had just been there. In fact, it was really odd because he suggested to Sinatra that he take me. I reckon Sinatra at first thought it was weird, too, but when my uncle mentioned something about, 'it was going to rain,' Sinatra took me by the arm and led me toward the door.

"'Come on, kid. Let's scram.'

"I found out later that that was the very day the Rangers finally busted the Maceo brothers and closed down the Balinese." Mickey then clasped his hands behind his head and leaned back into his chair, lifting the front legs off the ground. He smiled with satisfaction at his tale.

Dave looked at Zeek, and Zeek looked at Dave. They both just smiled and nodded.

XI

I'll Remember You No More

Dedicated to Laurie Jo

Standing looking down at the freshly turned earth as a slow drizzle begins, I struggle with the right words to make you understand what I am about to do. How can I tell you this is the only time I will visit you here? This is the only time I will speak to you or about you ever again. How can I make you understand that I am not strong enough to return to our memories? I will no longer tell anyone of the joy you brought into my life. I will never recount to anyone that it was I who became your lover and protector. How can I? The pain is too great, and all my strength is gone. From now on, I'll remember you no more.

Remembering those in our past is tricky for some. Many would say that—that to remember a loved one is to memorialize their life forever. That's what this strange old woman I'd never met told me at your funeral. She said even the difficult memories are somehow a tribute to the beauty of the departed one's life. But what she didn't say, what she needed to tell me, was how one deals with the pain that comes with remembering one who is no longer breathing next to you. How do you live with the pain of no more touching, no more holding, no more feeling the other inside—inside our hearts, inside our very souls? Oh, yeah, she said it is good to remember, to assist with closure.

I say bullshit.

Closure for me is forgetting all—both the bad and the good. Easy to let go of the bad, harder to give up the good, but the good only reminds me of what I lost. And that's too much pain for me.

Yeah, the old woman, she also told me that I was being selfish refusing to remember.

Again, I say bullshit!

I can't function properly when I remember you. Nothing gets done when all I can do is wail against the Roman Manes of the afterlife. Maybe it is just selfishness on my part; maybe it is just a sort of built-in protection from the tears. I know that you could do it. Maybe we should trade places; maybe it should be you throwing dirt on my face.

The rain is falling steadily now, dripping off my old, brown Fedora to my nose and then to the dirt, your dirt. I know you're looking up at me with those sightless eyes, and I know your silent voice is mocking me and my hat. You never did get that I was always looking to create my own sense of fashion.

I gotta be me, I would sing.

You gotta be Indiana Jones, you would respond.

And then you would smile, as I imagine you are doing so now way into eternity. You knew I would disagree and argue as I explained my hat to me represents the spirit of Hammett and Chandler—the private dicks of the 40s. You always giggled when I said private dick. I would explain I was more interested in solving life's mysteries than finding life's treasures. And yet, here I am, staring down at the one great mystery I could not solve, realizing the treasure I've lost forever.

Forgive me, but I just won't be able to remember you to anyone after today. I can't do it. I just can't pretend that you somehow still exist, if only in my memories. I've tried.

While we stood outside the chapel after the preacher said only the most excellent things about you, your friends all looked to me to reminisce about some time from your life that could lessen the sadness. Operating from someone else's social construct, I hesitantly recounted the time I acted as your personal avenger and smashed a trash can lid over Dale Small's head just for teasing you. You were only nine, and I couldn't handle your tears. No one, and I mean no one, was allowed to make you cry, not even my best friend Dale. He forever displayed the scar of remembrance since no hair ever grew there again. Your friends all laughed, and I imagined you did too as you lay there so close to me in that dark, gray box.

The laughter felt good, so I continued after winking at you in your box. I told them of the green-dyed apple dumplings, knowing you would be furious that I revealed your ornery side. You always complained that your fair share of the dumplings were gone before you got a chance to sit down and eat them, so you decided to dye them green one night, believing that the color would put your family off, and they wouldn't eat them. It worked, you told me, but you swore me to secrecy so that no one outside your immediate family would know you had an ornery bent when needed.

For a moment there, I was on a roll. I couldn't help myself, so without hesitation this time, I launched into the memory of when you lost the top half of your bathing suit due to an amorous wave, and I swam out to rescue you. I gave you my trunks to cover up with and then waited bobbing in the sea until you could bring me a towel. Still not sure why I didn't think of that first—bringing you a towel, but I thought of the act as noble nevertheless. You always smiled when I told that story and nodded in agreement that it was indeed was very noble. No one ever noticed the sly smile on your face as you remembered the act from a different perspective. You probably are doing it right now. I swear to you, my motives were gallant. I swear I wasn't trying to look! Your friends looked nervously at one another, wanting to know if it was appropriate at this time to laugh about your nakedness. I knew you would, indeed, laugh. You would laugh at me because you knew it would embarrass me. You always said my embarrassment was cute.

But today, I don't feel cute in your presence. Maybe it's because I already know what I am about to do. Turning away from my awkwardness there with your friends, I notice the old woman. She stood there next to the funeral's carriage that would soon carry you away to your last home. I thought she was there because she knew you, perhaps. As I brushed past her headed for the other car, she whispered, "Finish her voice."

Turning around, I asked, "Excuse me? Did you say something?"

"Finish her voice," she repeated quietly, looking down.

Her attire was unusual. She wore brightly colored and flowing scarves and lots of jewelry. She had a large turquoise ring on her left hand. Her skin was dark, but not from the sun. The many lines in her face revealed that hers was a life that lived in times knowing when to laugh and times when life held no laughter. Her grey hair was crowned with a large-brimmed hat with a fresh flower in the hatband. It looked like a flower plucked from one of your many arrangements. For the life of me, I could not place her inside the chapel. She then looked up at me with eyes so dark they seemed to be black, and they looked well past mine into my very soul. From under the brim of that hat, I noticed her tears and the red outline of those penetrating eyes. I averted mine partly so as not to embarrass her, and also because of my awkwardness, I looked toward you and asked, "I'm sorry, but how did you know her?"

Looking also to you, she moaned and then turned and spoke to me. "I know of her. I have stood here before like you do now. I know the weight we all take on when a voice goes silent." Turning again and looking back to you, she spoke like she was addressing you, but her words addressed me. "Finish her voice."

"What does that mean 'finish her voice'?"

Again, her eyes wrestled with mine, and pinning my attention so I could not run, she spoke softly and with sadness knowing her words were probably revealing something I would not fully understand.

She said, "We all have a voice in this existence that continues into the next. Our voices together complete a purpose. That purpose is a message that can guide us in this life and in service to one another. Whether that voice challenges this reality or helps the less mature voices to join in, we all must contribute to complete the message."

Looking back to you and then to me, she continued, "When a voice is taken away, it is up to the ones who remain to complete their message, up to us to finish their voice."

Turning and addressing you again, she said, "Her voice was not finished. she had young voices under her charge, and they need to hear from you."

Then turning back to me with her eyes now hidden under the lowered brim of her hat, she said, "Be her voice to her charges. Without it, they will suffer needlessly. They won't be able to find their way. They will not find their own voice. They cannot complete the message."

Starring at her with my mouth agape, I thought—What the hell! Message! Finish her voice! Charges! I had no idea what this crazy gypsy-like old lady was talking about, much less what she was doing here. She really didn't seem to know you, or at least she never offered any memory of you and her together. What was it she said, 'I know of her,' and not that she knew you? Did she read about you in the obits? Was she a friend of a friend? I looked back to you to ask these questions, and when I turned back to address them to the old woman, she was gone!

"Weird, huh? And you thought I was strange," I said out loud to your dirt.

The rain is pouring harder now. The brim of my Fedora is leaning more toward you with the weight of the water pulling it down, and a river of fallen rain is slowly eroding your dirt pile. Everyone has left you. You and I stand alone. Well, I stand, you, uh, you, never mind.

I'm delaying my final departure because I know it's the end for us, or perhaps—well, maybe it's just the end for me. I'm not sure how you are feeling about my decision to forget us. Or more clearly to forget you. Something that old woman said, she said you had charges? Who was she talking about? Was there someone else in your life that I didn't know about? Maybe—maybe she meant that the world would certainly miss your voice. Is that what she meant by finishing your voice? Did she really think that I could speak for you? Did she really think that I could complete your message—whatever the hell the message is! She was clearly mistaken if that was her meaning. Maybe she got the wrong casket. Maybe that's why I didn't see her in your service. That's it! She must have thought you were someone else. She was mistaken, right?

IT'S NOT MY RESPONSIBILITY! THE WORLD IS NOT MY CHARGE! I don't owe anybody nothin'! Let someone else finish your damn voice! If I tried, it would only remind me of you.

Sorry, I just can't do that. Please, don't make me do this! Find someone else.

Pssst. Look there to your left, three holes down. It looks like you will have company after all. There's a young woman with fresh tears putting fresh flowers on a fresh grave on this same row. She will have to pass by you to get to her memorial stone. There's a man's name on it. Maybe she will introduce you, that is if she doesn't mind telling her man he's lying near a beautiful young woman. She must be a military widow; the grave has one of those little flags that they put out on Veteran's Day. You know the kind you can buy for a quarter at the Dollar General.

I always wondered if a dead soldier wanted a remembrance of the country that got him this wonderful and forever ground-level view. They certainly have no say in the matter now. You always said I was being disrespectful. I say I was just being me. You knew I had buddies put here due to 'Nam. It wasn't their choice. And they always told me not to let anyone put those damn little flags on them. They said they didn't want to look up and be reminded of what country put them here. You would always roll your eyes at my unpatriotic resistance toward the government, saying the draft was long gone. Then you would flash those beautiful blues at me and smile that smile, and I would yield to your way of thinking. Yielding kept that often fragile cord between us for so long. But now I'm afraid that I have to let go of that cord. I just can't; I just can't. Maybe the guy a few holes down will be better company. Who knows, maybe he requested his flag.

I did fight one battle for you—the battle with God for your life here. Now you know that I believe in God, always have. And I know that it wasn't Him who released sickness and disease on this earth. That's on us and that other guy, that snake. But when God said He needed you more than me, I had to stand my ground. He already had so many, and I only had you. I couldn't understand how anyone or anything possibly could need you more than me. Still, near the end, you said you wanted to go. You even said He was coming for you. You said you could actually see Him in the corner of the hospital ceiling, standing with open arms, but I didn't see anything. You became agitated and began to shout as you pointed a shaky finger at the wall and shouted over and over, "I see Him! I see Him! Don't 'cha see Him?"

But I didn't see anything. You were so convinced that I turned and shouted out at the plaster, "YOU CAN'T HAVE HER! I'm not ready to let her go. Please! Please let her stay. Please!" I then stood ready to go toe to toe with the invisible Creator of the Universe. I know He could've squashed me like a bug; in fact, He probably thought about turning me into a bug so that I would crawl around and annoy others. Someone told me the Good Book says that death has no sting, but I disagree. It stung! It stung like hell! Nobody prepared me. I just simply wasn't prepared.

I lost that battle that day. I just wasn't strong enough or good enough to convince Him to let you stay. In the end, I'm kinda ok with that since you no longer are suffering. Guess that's the best for you, but what about me? Who's gonna heal me? Who's gonna hold me?

Well, I guess it's time to go. The rain's stopped, and my hat is all limp from the soaking. I've said all that I intended to say. I know that my argument is not strong enough to convince you why I can't ever return, but it is all I have. I will leave something with you, though. Something for you to remember me by. It's my grief. It's my memories.

I am burying them along with you.

XII

Quarantined

✦

"Here's all the pertinent information, including the latest photo that we have on file."

"Thanks. Where did you say I was going again?"

"Oklahoma. Some small town called, umm, let me see. It says it somewhere here; I just saw it. I remember when I read it, it sounded ironic. Batesville! Batesville, Oklahoma, you know, like the casket company. You gotta admit that's ironic, isn't it? Ha, ha. You get it—Batesville, the casket company, and you're going there too. Oh, never mind. It's a small town west of Elk City. Here's your rental car information. And I found you a motel with the attached garage like you like. It's called the Park and Rest Inn. You pick up your rental car from Avis. Say, aren't you originally from Oklahoma?"

"Yeah, Guymon, out in the panhandle, but I haven't been back there in a long, long time. See you when I get back, Gracie."

"See ya, Jack. Be careful and wear your damn mask! Batesville, ha, that's so ironic. Batesville!"

He drove for almost eleven hours the second day to try and get to the motel before midnight. He felt awfully tired from the drive. Usually, long drives didn't bother him; perhaps he was coming down with something. Who knows nowadays, with the pandemic and all. Maybe it was just bad coffee from that little gas station convenience store. Looked like the coffee had been sitting there for some time. Or maybe he caught something from the elderly man behind the counter who was coughing and complaining of a headache. Gracie told Jack to wear his mask, but he just couldn't get the hang of the habit.

From somewhere long ago, Jack told the old man to go home and get some rest. He hated that folks couldn't retire on what they earned in life but had to keep working. He remembered his old man struggling all the way into retirement, and Jack still had to make ends meet for him. Because of his dad's pride, he had to get pretty creative to get the money to him. It seems Jack's dad believed he was endeared to many minor relatives that he'd nearly forgotten, but they remembered him with many small inheritances. Jack never told anyone 'til he was alone at the tombstone.

Of course, Jack never thought about retiring, even though he could have many years ago. No, he would keep on working until someone else decided it was time for him to go. In his business, that's how it was done. He would be retired.

With the shopkeeper's brass bell announcing Jack's arrival, the lady behind the counter looked up from her newspaper. She said, "Welcome to the Park and Rest Inn. What can I help you with?"

He looked up at her, shaking his head in disbelief about the remarkable resemblance she had to Alice, the Brady Bunch's housekeeper. He had the sudden urge to ask which room Marsha was staying in, but he resisted temptation knowing that she probably had heard it all before. She breathed in long and slow and then released her breath as she lowered her shoulders and smiled, knowing from all these years what a customer thought when they first saw her.

Jack smiled back; her name tag said, *Alice.*

Shaking off his fatigue, Jack said in a lowered voice from under his dark brown trilby, "Got a smoker with attached garage?"

Jack always lowered his voice just like he lowered his head when talking to anyone who might have the occasion to remember him. He never looked them directly in the eye either, a habit he instituted many years ago when he started in the business. He prided himself as the one person in a room no one ever remembered. He learned this from a contemporary. This is probably why he's lasted so long, that and careful planning.

Alice asked, looking at her registration book, "Is there more than one or just you?"

"Just me," he said quietly with an awkward smile and a quick glance at her from under the trilby brim.

The lights were off as he stepped into the room. Experience led him to the light switch, and he gave the room his usual inspection locating any additional exits. He saw through an open bathroom door a small window, but big enough in a hurry. Throwing his suitcase on the bed with the faded yellow ripcord bedspread, he surveyed the rest of the room. He placed his satchel with the envelope Gracie had given him on the chair next to the bathroom door. He decided to wait till morning to look it over; all he wanted was sleep. One thing he noticed immediately was the tidiness of the room. Jack always appreciated a clean room. There were even fresh flowers on the desk attached to the wall next to the dresser/credenza where an out-of-place, updated flat-screen TV sat. He dropped his wallet, keys, and phone on the desk. Jack made a mental note to leave the maid a good tip.

It was too late to go into town to get something decent to eat, so Jack just headed back to the lobby to peruse the snack machine and get a soda. He had a bottle of Old Forester that would do fine with a Coke. He figured a good night's sleep would shake the weariness and put him back on track. Jack rubbed his temples and scanned the other machines for some Bayer aspirin. He thought a dollar in quarters was pretty pricey for two aspirins. Then wiping the sweat from his brow, he put another two quarters into another machine and selected a Mound's bar, thinking that was the healthiest the machine could offer. After all, it had coconut in it.

Unlocking the door, Jack remembered he had forgotten to fill his ice bucket. He usually was more efficient with his movements. Grabbing the ice bucket, he headed back to the ice machine near the lobby. Man, he was exhausted; he just wanted to get some whiskey in him and hit the sack. He again wiped the sweat from his brow as he turned the doorknob and then realized he had not locked the door. Sloppy! Jack thought he better pull it together if this business was to come off without a hitch.

Back in the room, he felt as if everything was spinning, and he fell on the bed, dropping the ice bucket on the low pile, gray carpeted floor. He thought as he lay there that he was too exhausted to move. Putting his hand to his forehead, Jack felt he had a fever. Then he remembered nothing as the darkness that always accompanied him took charge.

Was he dreaming? Jack felt someone was in the room. It brought him instinctively to a crouched position by the side of the bed. He knew if someone had gotten in, they would have the advantage in his confused and weakened state. His clothes were soaked from a night of sweat, as were his sheets. Jack now noticed his still present fever was accompanied by last night's headache, which didn't come from a night of whiskey. If he had been drinking, then he would have something to blame for feeling so shitty. A persistent knocking was coming from the motel door that seemed convinced of his presence. Jack then heard:

"Housekeeping. Is anyone in there?"

Turning slowly to the door from his squatted defense, he saw the handle beginning to turn and then stood up, looking for his satchel. Whoever was coming in was not going to get past the threshold if he made it to his satchel. But his fever located his bag miles away across the room in a chair, so he moved to the door and leaned his shoulder into it to prevent its opening.

With a lot of effort, Jack managed to speak through the door, "I'm feeling a bit sick. Probably a cold or some kinda' flu. Don't think it would be good to come in to clean right now. Better to be safe with all the crap goin' on."

There was a silence for what seemed like hours on the other side, and finally, in a heavily accented voice that surely came from beautiful lips, "Ok, Señor. I will leave the towels and sheets outside here in case you need them. I will come back mañana."

Sliding down to the floor with his back against the door, Jack felt fatigued, drained of any energy to stand and walk to the bathroom. Thinking a shower might revive him, he decided to just sit there for a bit more and let the coolness coming in from under the door bathe him.

Bathe! Jack remembered Saturday nights in Guymon when his grandmother would fill the horse trough with fresh creek water, just like in her youth. She always sent him first ahead of his brothers and sisters for this weekend bath. Jack always assumed it was because he was the favored. His grandmother insisted he bathe on Saturday night so he would be clean for church in the morning. She would always oversee the ritual and admonish Jack to scrub the sin away. His grandmother always washed his clothes on Saturday, too, so he always felt they were a little stiff putting them on. He remembered the fresh smell of sunshine on his shirt sleeve. Still sitting and leaning against the motel door, Jack absently raised his arm to his nose to revisit the smells but noticed there were none. He sniffed again, but again nothing! He couldn't smell the past or the present. Remembering, he sniffed the room for the freshness, but nothing.

Odd.

Crawling slowly to the nightstand by the bed, he fumbled for the TV remote. Turning it on, Jack thought breaking the silence would help him feel better. He ran the channels 'til he landed on CNN and decided some updates from around the country would take his mind off his strange sickness. Deciding his position on the floor was fine, he leaned against the wall watching the newscasters read their scripts. It seemed all they could talk about was the pandemic and the flu virus COVID-19. Jack listened to the drone of the reporter's voice as he read from his paper cheat sheet:

The CDC reports that "people with COVID-19 have had a wide range of symptoms reported – ranging from mild symptoms to severe illness. Symptoms may appear 2-14 days after exposure to the virus. People with these symptoms may have COVID-19: fever or chills, cough, shortness of breath or difficulty breathing, fatigue, muscle or body aches, headache, new loss of taste or smell, sore throat, congestion or runny nose, nausea or vomiting, diarrhea. This list does not include all possible symptoms. CDC will continue to update this list as we learn more about COVID-19." We will keep you updated when more breaks on this pandemic. Back to you, Brianna.

COVID?

Jack shook his head in disbelief. He thought I don't have no damn COVID! I haven't been around anybody. Been stuck in a car for the last two days. Wait a minute! The old man at the convenience store. But that was yesterday. The TV said it takes two or more days for symptoms to manifest. Two days ago, I was talking to Gracie. Gracie! I gotta' call Gracie. Now she'll rag on me about not being religious wearing that damn mask, but it was just that one-time getting coffee, and I kept my distance. Yeah, I gotta' call Gracie, Jack thought as his head nodded from exhaustion. And then…he…fell…asleep.

"Señor. It is housekeeping. Are you ok, Señor?" the beautiful lips demanded from the other side of the door.

Waking to the persistent knocking but too weak to defend, Jack found himself still leaning against the wall on the floor. He had fallen asleep upright and woke with a pain in his neck from his chin leaning on his chest. Blurry-eyed, he eyed the door and hoped it held, keeping him safe until he was able to defend again.

"Señor, I worry for you. Is there perhaps something I can do?"

Jack pushed himself up using the wall as support, and as if for the first time, he walked tentatively to the door. Leaning against it, he spoke through it to his angel of mercy, "I have some kind of flu or sickness, and I don't want you to catch it. So I think it best that we keep the door closed until I feel better."

For the first time, Jack noticed the peephole in the door, and he slowly moved his eye to view his angel. Even through the distortion of the rounded effect of the glass, he could tell this woman was very beautiful. He quickly noticed her dark hair was pulled back and tucked neatly to the back of her head. She wore a maid's uniform of pale blue that accentuated her curves. Jack thought that either she was proud of those curves, or she wore a uniform provided by the motel management for someone much smaller. Still, the uniform was pressed as if to say *I am proud of what I do.* At that moment, Jack wished he could say the same.

"Maybe, maybe I should bring you some soup, si? Have you food to eat?"

Just above a weakened whisper, Jack replied, "Haven't had anything but a Mounds bar since I got here. Not even sure I finished that." He scanned the room for the evidence and located the candy bar still unopened next to where the ice bucket would have been set on the dresser. He wondered where the ice bucket was and then saw it still on the floor amidst a wet spot. Jack made a mental note that he had better clean that up before he let Angel Lips in.

"I will make you soup and leave it here outside your door. It will be good for your sickness. I will be back pronto, Señor."

Jack just slid down the door and sat with his back against it. He began to wonder where the chairs were. He was glad the carpets were kept clean. Jack made a mental note not to sit or lay down near the ice bucket as he drifted back into darkness.

It didn't take long for him to be back in Guymon. He was sitting on the hard wooden pew listening to an old man with white hair that seemed to be growing out of his ears. The man was yelling while emphasizing with his finger at individuals and simply saying:

"YOU! and YOU! and YOU! CONFESS YOUR SINS AND

TURN FROM YOUR WICKED WAYS!"

When the finger was turned on him, Jack shrunk back into the pew, trying to avoid the stares from the congregation, which he was convinced all turned toward him. He looked up in horror at his grandmother, who was agreeing with the preacher and shouting, "Amen!" and "Halleluiah!" all while rattling a tambourine and keeping beat with stomping feet.

A soft knock at the door startled Jack gladly back to the present. He could barely hear his angel of mercy and prayed he could stand and gaze at her once again through the peephole.

"I leave now. Drink soup while it's hot. Good for you. I will be back mañana. Take care, Señor."

When he finally stood erect, Jack searched through the peephole and saw her as she walked away. The further away she got, the less distortion, although the curves remained.

When she was out of sight, he opened the door carefully and, with shaking hands, pulled the tray inside. She had wrapped a couple of homemade tortillas in a cloth napkin along with a bowl of steaming soup covered by tin foil. The food looked delicious, and he felt it was made with care, but Jack couldn't taste or smell any of it.

No one had made him soup in a long, long time.

It's funny how there are noises we hear while we sleep, and we are not quite sure if they are noises in our dreams or from somewhere outside of sleep. Jack swore he was hearing a phone ringing, but he couldn't identify from where. He awoke with every part of his body aching, and he noticed it was hard to catch his breath. It probably didn't help that he had passed out on the floor again. Pushing himself up into a sitting position with his arms was difficult. His arms were usually strong for his business; however, not today. As Jack scanned the room again, trying to orient his senses, he realized he could still hear a phone ringing. The sound was coming from the desk near the TV. Grabbing the doorknob, he pulled himself up and moved unsteadily to where he had dropped his keys and wallet the day before. The screen on his phone said, "Gracie."

"Jack, you ok? I never heard from you when you checked in. That's so unlike you. Do you feel ok?"

Jack took a moment to respond, and when he did, it was again no more than a whisper, "No, I got some kinda' flu, I think. It's kickin' my ass."

"It's the flu, alright. I tested positive today for COVID. I've been calling you all morning since I found out. You got it bad?"

"Yeah."

"Well, stay put. We both got to quarantine for a couple of weeks. What symptoms are you showing?"

"According to the TV, I got 'em all. Say Darlin', I thought you were keeping yourself safe. What happened to Miss Wear Your Damn Mask? If I live through this, I'm gonna kick your butt!"

Waiting a moment to admit fault, Gracie finally said, "Well, it seems there was this one guy. Jack, I am so sorry. You are right; it's all on me. I deserve to have my butt kicked. What can I do for you from this end? Do you think you need to go to the hospital?" and lowering her voice even though they were talking on the phone, she whispered, "Have you done the job yet?"

"I haven't been out of this damn motel room since I drove in the other night. I haven't even opened the envelope. I got some motel maid bringing me soup and leaving it outside the damn door. Gracie, you may need to get someone else to make this hit. If the client is in a hurry, call Big Tuna and get him to—"

Interrupting him, Gracie said with a sympathy she kept

hidden for the man she had known for the last twenty some odd years, "Jack, don't worry about the contract. It's being handled. I've been in contact with the client and told him you had road trouble, and he's cool with it for now. He said he wanted you to do it. It seems he's used you in the past and likes your work. So, lay low, get well and eat plenty of soup. And be sure to leave that maid a good tip. I'll be in touch. Oh, and Jack, again, I am so sorry."

In Jack's line of business, he relied on his trained ability to observe and react quickly. But this COVID thing had dulled his senses and slowed his reactions. Normally he would have noticed the shadow moving under the door and would have positioned himself defensively long before the knock. Jack hadn't lasted this long in the business by being sloppy. But the soft knock at the door surprised him, and he turned slowly toward the sound, wondering if in that instant it meant danger and would require quick thinking, which for the life of him he was not able to summon at this very moment. Then he smiled, knowing this was his Angel Lips.

"Señor, pardon Señor, I worry for you all night. What can I do for you this day? How can I help?"

Moving to the door and stealing a look through the peephole, Jack gathered his voice to respond, "That soup was wonderful! I haven't had homemade soup since I was a kid. Thank you. You are so kind to do that for me."

"Mi Madre—my mother—she teach me how to make good soup. I'm glad that it pleased you. I will bring you some more, Señor. But what else can I do for you? The towels and sheets are still here at the door. Maybe I can come in and change them for you?"

"No! I believe I have the COVID," Jack said with labored

breath. "I don't want to expose you. I'll get the sheets after you leave."

She reacted when he mentioned COVID and backed away from the door, frowning. Again the peephole distortion lessened, and he could see just how lovely her voice agreed with her features. At that moment, he cursed Gracie and the damn COVID. Usually, Jack avoided relationships when he was working to keep his senses sharp, but this woman was a temptation that he could not have resisted. For a brief moment, he considered opening the door and inviting her in but then gained control of his lusts and decided protecting her was the ultimate sacrifice.

"As you wish, Señor. I will come back with more soup."

Watching her walk away, Jack imagined a different time and a different place. As the fatigue took over and he slowly slipped to the floor once again, he wondered what she smelled like. He imagined she had a freshness that complimented the room as he remembered that first night. He thought how wonderful it would be to run his fingers through her dark hair as he loosened it from the back of her head. His last thought was of her lips. Those lips that first captured his guarded emotions. Those lips, those lips...

"Jack! Come here this instant! Are you the one who made this mess?" his grandmother demanded.

He knew what was coming. He knew because it happened time and time again. The cinch strap that hung by the front door had long forgotten how to hold a saddle. But it never forgot how to bring the blood. Jack wondered how this woman who loved Jesus so much on Sundays could be the devil the rest of the week. He was eleven years old and the only one of his siblings who stayed behind while the others ran away. Well, not this time! The punishment never seems to match the crime. This time Jack would stand up to his grandmother. This time the outcome would be different. This time he would be older.

"You ain't hittin' me with that cinch again! I'll clean up the mess, but you ain't gonna beat me ever again!"

"Why, you little impertinent bastard! You come here this minute and take your punishment. The Bible says, 'spare the rod, spoil the child.' I ain't having no rebellious child under my roof. Now your folks done run off and left you in my care, and I aim to see you grow respectable and obedient like my folks did me. Your brothers and sister they all done runoff and made their decision to travel the pathway to Hell. I ain't about to let that happen to you, you understand! I will beat the hell out of you until you're just like Jesus—without sin! With the help of God and Pastor Jenkins, I promise you I will. Now come here this instant!"

"No, ma'am, you ain't gonna beat me," and with his bold declaration, Jack grabbed a large pickle crock and smashed it into his grandmother's skull, dropping her instantly. The blood ran across the freshly scrubbed floor planks until it reached his bare feet. Jack thought for a moment that his grandmother, if she could, would certainly be mad as hell at this mess. He turned to the door but hesitated, and over his shoulder, he spoke to the body lying crumpled on the wood floor, "No one's ever gonna beat me again. No one!"

Now Pastor Jenkins considered himself a man of God, and it was his business to whip his congregation into shape when needed. He even assisted widowed mothers in disciplining their hard-to-control children by holding them down while their momma beat them. A good child is an obedient child, he would shout over the children's screams and protestations. After sending the bruise and broken children to their rooms to huddle in the darkness alone, Pastor Jenkins would invite himself to supper, and often stayed until after breakfast.

"Jack, how can I help you? How's your grandmother these days?" Pastor Jenkins asked, surprised at the tall boy standing in his doorway. The pastor thought to himself that this young boy would soon be a strapping young man and would grow to be a real help to his grandmother, working the land for her. He then noticed the boy was carrying a leather cinch strap. He'd seen it before.

"I aim to kill you for helpin' beat me. You ain't never gonna beat no kid ever again."

That was the second time Jack killed, and he did so without regret.

Jack began to look forward to the soft knock at his motel door. He was surprised he even heard it through his troubled sleep. Maybe she was becoming the one good thing in his life, and he never wanted to miss any of it. He had missed so much growing up. Jack had found his dad later in his life, but his mother was already lying under a marker. Again pulling himself up with the help of the doorknob, Jack thought he ought to spend more time closer to the bed.

"Señor, I have brought more soup, and I brought a bottle of tequila as well. Mi padre says tequila is good for the soul. I think it might be good for the sickness, too. Are you feeling better, Señor? Is the soup helping? Are you resting well? Can I get you some medicine for the fever and headache?"

Jack realized she had educated herself on COVID symptoms and smiled at her concern and thoughtfulness. Speaking to the wood barrier between them, he asked, "What is your name?"

"Angelina," she said, lowering her eyes, aware that this man must be looking at her through the door.

As he watched her eyes, he imagined she was shy about her amazing loveliness. Jack was certain many men had flattered her with words that never could quite express her beauty.

"Angelina. That is a beautiful name. Angelina. Let's see, in the Greek, it means angel or messenger of God. You certainly are my angel these last couple of days. I don't imagine I would have survived if not for you. Thank you, Angelina," Jack said slowly and with labored breathing.

"It is nothing, Señor. I do this gladly. You have a kind voice," and she blushed, sneaking a look at the peephole. She longed to see the other side. Perhaps this man would be different. He certainly sounded like he was. And he liked her soup. It had been a while since anyone had complimented her, even if it was just soup. She smiled to herself—imagining.

Sliding a new one hundred dollar bill under the door, Jack said, "Take this, Angelina. You have spent your own money helping me, and I want to repay you."

Pushing the money back inside, she replied with sincerity, "No, Señor. It is nothing, what I do. I do not do this for the money. Keep the money, por favor."

"I insist. You paid for the tequila. I can see it is not opened. Please, this would make me happy. Please!"

Conscientious that he could see so clearly through the door the unopened bottle, she smoothed her dress, pressing it more tightly against her body, "Very well, Señor. But I shall go and bring you some medicine for the headache with this money. Is there anything else you perhaps would like?"

Hesitating, knowing it was not possible at present to say what he really wanted to say, Jack said, "Angelina, keep the money for yourself. Don't worry about me. Let me show you how much you mean to me and express my gratitude for your kindness. Keep the money for yourself. And by the way, my name is Jack, not Señor. Please call me Jack."

Smiling, she looked right through the door, "Very well, Jack. I will return." Then with slow, deliberate movements, Angelina smiled and walked away. Jack, too smiled as the distortion faded once again.

Lying down this time on the bed after spreading out the sheets Angelina had left at the door (he was too exhausted to tuck them in or remove the older ones), Jack let the fever take him back to the memories that shaped him. Funny the things one remembers, he thought. Why were there no happy memories? When he closed his eyes, all he saw was blood. All his life, there was blood, either his or others. And there were so many others. Then through the blood, he saw Angelina, his angel. For her, he thought, he would end this life of killing for others. He imagined she could love him away from the blood that made him and others like him necessary.

Jack remembered that Pastor Jenkins talked about blood, and he would yell that God demanded justice as he pounded his bible on the wood pulpit. Jack had convinced himself he was God's justice toward those who brought evil into the world, no matter how minor. Justice to those who stole from others, justice to those who killed indiscriminately, justice to those who hurt children. They all deserved God's justice, and Jack brought that justice. Right? Without justice, there would be no absolutes, he thought. No absolutes, and there would be chaos. Right? Jack thought the world needed him. He believed God needed him, and he hoped that Angelina would come to need him too.

Trying to avoid the cliché every man in this business thought, Jack wondered where was the justice for him. His young life was stolen from him, and his grandmother taught him love was a beating. Jack avoided love and relationships for many reasons. He was constantly told that any relationships in this business could cost you an advantage or, worse, get you killed. He wondered if he could love without beating? But, he also wondered if there ever was a time the rules didn't hold. Could he escape with Angelina? Could she change his memories? He never really knew love, but he liked to think that loving a woman was like smoking a fine cigar or a shot of good whiskey. The rolling between your fingers, the smell, the taste, and the feel, those were his only tangible feelings of love. He needed Angelina to help him to real love.

Several days passed, Jack wasn't really sure how many while the fever raged. Every day Angelina brought him soup and aspirin. She spoke softly through the door, causing him to desire her more and more. She left clean sheets, and Jack just piled them one on top of the other, being too sick to make the bed. He hadn't showered since he'd arrived. Then one morning after a fitful night, the fever broke. Jack's pile of sheets smelled of sweat and urine. Smelled! He could smell again. And speaking of, he decided he was long overdue for a shower. Exhausted, he showered and shaved and then gathered the sheets in a pile by the door. He wasn't immediately sure of what to do with them. Jack felt a sense of embarrassment dumping these sheets on Angelina. He looked through the peephole to see if she was anywhere near. Carefully opening the door and looking both ways slowly, he gathered up the sheets and carried them to the dumpster at the end of the row of rooms.

The effort left him drained of any more energy, and he collapsed into a chair that held his satchel. Dropping the satchel on the floor, Jack noticed the envelope inside containing the mark's information. Curious, he opened it to see who his assignment was.

Pulling out the photo, he immediately knew those brown eyes, those angel lips.

Horrified, Jack quickly scanned the info sheet that stated justification. Jack demanded that Gracie always include the justification for the hit. If he was to be God's justice, he needed to know why. He read that Angelina was a former girlfriend for a cartel boss. She had escaped him and had taken a large amount of money as well as a transaction ledger. The boss wanted the ledger back, and he wanted Angelina dead. He wanted justice, so he called for Jack.

The familiar soft knock at the door startled him, and he dropped the envelope back into his satchel. Rising slowly with this new information, Jack realized his sense of justice and his sense of love would not be allowed to coexist. Slowly opening the door to Angelina's surprised smile as she stepped back in caution.

"Fever broke sometime last night or this morning. I think it's safe to come in," Jack said without a smile. He opened the long-held wooden barrier that had kept them distant for so long. Angelina stepped tentatively over the threshold, looking backward as Jack shut the door, leaving them for the first time alone, both on the same side. He stepped around her and smelled the lovely freshness of her subtle perfume. He had never smelled anything so wonderful in his life. Jack bent down and picked up his satchel.

"I'm headed home, Gracie."
 "Did you bring justice?"
 Jack wasn't sure how to answer.

XIII

The Cowboy and the Hippy Chick

I was born from whiskey; I was named from whiskey. That's what you get when your pa's a drunkard. He bred my mom one night after a tent revival meetin'. Who else but the devil his self could convince a young virgin to slip out into the darkness after hearin' about how heaven ain't for whoremongers and deceitful liars? Who else but a drunkard—out of meanness—would name their boy Spurious Gustafurd Hendershot? Who else but a drunkard?

A rusty, dented Ford pickup pulled into the Dairy Mart parking lot, pulling an old cattle trailer full of gathered winter calves fat for auction. The driver parked across several parking spaces at the back of the lot so as to get the trailer out of the line of the lunch crowd traffic. Out of the cab jumped a cowboy who was sprier than his age seemed to indicate. Just how old, no one knew for sure. He said he was born around 1900, but he wasn't certain. His mother died soon after birthing him, and no one ever gave him a party. All his pa gave him was a name and a shove out the door when he was around twelve, along with the words, "You're old enough to make it on your own. Now get." He had seen sixty or more winters since making it out west.

As his boot leather scratched the asphalt, he gathered up his jeans that, if it had not been for the suspenders and belt, would have slipped down over his hips. He thought it was time to put on some winter weight too. Just then, a black GTO full of rambunctious teenage boys roared through the parking lot and swerved dangerously close to the cowboy. Laughing, they sped out onto the highway leaving the air full of foul-smelling burning rubber and a trail of black tire marks. The cowboy pulled his hat and slapped his legs to wipe off the dust and dirt while thinking a mesquite switch could be put to good use right now. There was a time, he remembered, that fools like this wouldn't be tolerated. He grinned, thinking about the time Johnny Drake got locked up by Sheriff Musgrave for throwing a mad skunk into the schoolhouse just to get out of taking a test. Sheriff Musgrave made sure Johnny took the test in jail, and then he had to scrub down the schoolhouse.

Yes, sir, the old cowboy thought a good mesquite switch would come in mighty handy right now. Meanwhile, from the fast-food restaurant, you could hear a female employee yelling at the boys from the side door. Then she noticed the old cowboy dusting himself off and hollered, "Spur's here; better get his order on. Remember, just take the moo out of his burger."

Spur had been stopping at the Dairy Mart when he came to town for the cattle sale for as long as anyone could remember. He always ordered the same thing—a burger cooked rare, twice-fried fries and a large chocolate malt with 3 extra shots of chocolate. The manager didn't seem to mind Spur asking for special consideration when it came to the menu; some had heard that the cowboy came to the aid of the manager's father many years ago. However, he was a stickler for the rules for everyone else. The menu had to be followed exactly, or there would be consequences. Why even the frozen dairy treats have to be weighed.

The story told locally was there was a counter boy who rebelled against the system and made banana splits too big during a frozen treat sale because he believed weighed treats oppressed the working class. The manager had been called in to bring more bananas because of the increased sales. He was delighted that his proposed split special was doing so well until he arrived and saw several humongous banana boats go by. He flew into a rage in front of the customers and sent the counter boy to the backroom and ordered him to finish his shift cleaning out the walk-in cooler. Afterward, the manager fired the free-thinking worker and banned him from ever setting foot on the property again. They say to this day, the counter boy wanders from town to town looking for a Dairy Mart that won't eject him once he sets foot on the property, or at the least make him a non-weighted banana split to go.

Hanging his hat on the back of his chair, Spur took his usual seat by the front window, so he could watch the traffic as it went by on ol' highway 87. He wasn't quite sure if the increased traffic was because the highway had gone from a dirt path to a paved road or if there were just more people out driving somewhere nowadays. Progress bothered Spur, but he thought it don't matter none no how. Time ain't gonna go backward, but that didn't mean he had to ride along with it. Sitting and staring out the window, he remembered when he moseyed along that dusty dirt path on a tall bay and pushed cattle to the sale rather than driving them in a trailer. Life wasn't simpler then, nor was it easier; it was just life.

Spur's attention was drawn to a dirty white Falcon as it pulled over to the side of the road to let a hitchhiker out. She was a young thing, he thought as he squinted his eyes in the hot afternoon sun. One of those hippy-looking chicks he heard folks talking about nowadays. Her hair was long and dark, and tied around her head was a colorful beaded headband with feathers. Maybe she thought she was Indian, Spur mused. There were more beads hanging around her neck, and the weight of them forced the small calico-flowered print shirt between her young breasts as they bounced freely and unrestrained. He wondered why young girls didn't wear bras anymore. He wondered what their daddies thought. The bell-bottom jeans she wore were too long for her, but she had managed to drag most of the back of the legs that hung over sandaled feet. With the many patches sewed on, Spur figured that these jeans not only were favored but probably the only pair the young girl owned.

Reaching into the back seat of the Falcon for a worn-out Army duffle bag and throwing it over her shoulder, she hollered back at the driver, thanking him for the ride, and, flashing a peace sign, headed toward the Dairy Mart. Just then, the black GTO roared past, going the other way with the horn blaring and the boys all hanging out and yelling from the windows.

The hippy chick appeared not to notice their hormonal flirtations and crude expressions as she stepped into the restaurant, but she was muttering something under her breath as she dropped the duffle bag near the front door and headed to the counter. The cowboy admired her spunk. The counter girl looking up to see who had just entered, said a little too loud over her shoulder, "Well, lookie here what just walked in. The circus must be in town." The hippy chick just smiled. It was not the first time she had heard that line.

"Spur, your order's ready," the counter girl yelled to the cowboy. Thanking her as he picked up his red plastic tray, Spur nodded to the hippy chick, and she flashed him a big smile that said she was living life by her design, not someone's expected plan for her age. He thought it's not easy carving out a path that some say has vanished or is just plain foolish. How many times had he heard—from well-meaning folks—that the cowboy life is dead? For Spur, the cowboy life was his path, even if that path had been paved.

As Spur sat down, he overheard her order: a burger with all the fixings—hold the burger—and a banana split. The counter girl yelled back at the grill cook with a little disgust in her voice for a vegetarian thingy. Peeking up over the counter, separating him from the customers at the pretty girl, the grill cook gave her a grin as he repeated her order for one burger all the way, hold the beef and one banana split. Spur moved his attention back to his meal and bowed his head out of gratitude for the life he loved all so well and thanked the Man upstairs for simple pleasures. While taking his first sip of the triple chocolate malt, a voice as lovely as the first spring flowers on a mountainside pasture asked to join him. Turning in her direction, Spur again saw that big smile and rose as he indicated to the chair across from him.

"Yes, ma'am. 'Preciate the company," he smiled as he nodded.

Extending her hand, the lovely voice said, "Name's Meadow. Don't believe I ever met a real live cowboy before." Grinning, she asked, "Is your horse tied out back?"

Her intent at teasing was lost on Spur as he replied, "No, ma'am. Some horses spook in town with all the traffic and such. Came to town in the Ford yonder," he said, pointing one of the several crooked fingers broken from too many ropings to where he had parked. "Been a while since I rode to town. Do miss it tho'. Easier to enjoy the flowers."

"Oh, the flowers! Aren't they far out, man!"

Puzzled, Spur responded, "Well, many of them grow right there on the side of the road, but guess you might could wander far out into the fields and be among 'em."

Meadow's slight smile made Spur think that he wasn't quite understanding what she was saying. It didn't matter to him as long as she just kept smiling. It had been many years since he felt this way in the company of a young lady. Too many years.

"So, ma'am, you just passin' through town, or you got folks nearby?"

"Nah…no folks. My ol' man split years ago, and my ol' lady she don't care about nothin' but her next martini. I'm just out diggin' life. Headed to the Haight eventually, you know out in California, but for now, just out thumbin', seein' where it takes me," pausing and staring out the window and then looking back into Spur's eyes, she exclaimed, "I get to sleep every night under the stars. Everything is so much more groovy when your soul is free to be! Besides, I'm a Sagittarian—we wander."

Again, Spur couldn't make sense of her words. Perhaps she was from another country. Didn't she say she was from Sagittaria? She probably still hadn't mastered the local lingo. He understood most folks and even knew a little Spanish from that time he worked down on the border, but this girl was something he had never run across. That's what happens when you only come to town once a month or so. Things change. Spur never saw the need to keep up with the changes.

The grill cook interrupted Spur's thoughts as he brought Meadow her order personally—a meatless burger and one extra-large banana split. The old cowboy smiled, recognizing the attempt to impress the hippy chick. And why not? She was as pretty as a newborn pup. The grill cook asked if there was anything else she needed, and she smiled that smile and told him everything looked "copacetic," especially the frozen delight. He knew he was risking banishment from the Dairy Mart, but he thought she was worth the firing. Grinning while spinning on his heels, his sneakers squeaked, leaving him embarrassed that his grand gesture now lacked the intended flirt.

The counter girl snickered.

He shot her the bird.

As Meadow bit into her meatless burger, Spur noticed the beauty of her sun-ripened skin and eyes as blue as a deep-spring-fed watering hole. It reminded him of that summer many years ago in northern Wyoming when he herded a string of unbroken ponies to that pool by a waterfall. He thought then that was one of the most beautiful places on earth until now. Spur thought it strange how he was feeling at the moment. What was it about Meadow that intrigued him so? He generally spent his time alone and without the company of women. Goodness, he was old enough to be this girl's grandpa! But still, he found himself attracted.

"You got a little ketchup on the corner of your mouth there," Meadow said, pointing, handing Spur a napkin.

"I don't never use no ketchup, ma'am," he replied as Meadow cocked her head at him for a moment and then opened her mouth wide in horror as she realized what the red was.

With disgust in her voice, she lowered her eyes and began, "You know if you must eat animals, you should have the decency to kill them first!" Raising her eyes and looking straight into Spur's, she continued, "Animals have a spirit too, you know."

Spur studied her for the longest time before he responded with all the kindness he could muster, "Ma'am, I knowed that animals have a spirit. The Lakota Sioux taught me that long ago, but creatures also have a purpose here on this 'yer earth. Some's for workin', and some's for feedin', and some's for just plain company. Now you take this 'yer cow I'm a eatin', its purpose is to feed folks' belly and to make them good boots to walk around in. I ain't a killin' no cow what I don't give thanks to the one who made it. And that's just how I see things." Spur waited for her to respond. He half expected her to bang him over the head with her red plastic tray or dump her soda in his lap, but she did neither. She just lowered her head as her lip began to tremble.

Looking up at him with water in the corners of her blue eyes, she attempted a slight smile before she began. "I don't mean no disrespect, Mister. I just see things differently, too. You see, I believe that there's a spirit in everything. There's a spirit in people, and I believe that that same spirit is in the animals and plants and trees and even in the rocks scattered on the ground. It's all around us, even in the air we breathe."

Pondering the hippy chick's response, Spur chose his words deliberately, "Well, ma'am, I don't know 'bout all that. I for one ain't never seen no rock bowed its head in the church house before, but I think that the Maker up yonder what made all this 'yer stuff got a little of that heavenly nature in all he—or she—done made." Spur gave her a respectful grin with those last few words. He then leaned back in his chair and couldn't help but tease a little bit as he asked, "Say, ma'am, how's that spirit a tastin' in that there tomater 'yer a eatin'?"

Stopping in mid-bite and then grinning, Meadow flashed him a peace sign and declared, "Truce."

As they finished their meal, their conversation lessened, and Spur began to notice the music coming from the grill cook's radio. It was B. J. Thomas and his song "Hooked on a Feeling."

The old cowboy smiled at the idea of experiencing that emotion again with Meadow when suddenly the next song startled him to his core as the singer, Gary Puckett, sang about a girl that was too young to be romanced.

Frightened of his thoughts, the old cowboy pushed his chair back away from the table as he rose slowly. Eyeing the girl deliberately, Spur realized his young buck days were long gone, so something else must be causing these stirrings. Curious, he did something that took him completely by surprise. While reaching for his hat, he extended his hand and offered, "Ma'am, you're a welcome to bed down out at my place. I'll throw in some breakfast, that is if'n you can tolerate some skillet biscuits and honey. Even build us a pot of coffee. What'd ya' say?"

Holding on to his rough, calloused hand with all its crooked fingers, Meadow smiled her wonderful smile, and then narrowing her eyes at Spur, she asked, "Just what do you mean by 'bed down'?"

Embarrassed by the thought that Meadow misunderstood his offer of friendship and puzzled that she would even entertain such a proposition, the cowboy lowered his head thinking. As he fiddled with his hat, he raised his eyes to look into hers and responded, "Ma'am, I didn't intend no shenanigans. Just offerin' a place to sleep the night. Hope that you didn't think I was proposin'..."

Laughing at his awkwardness, Meadow said she would love to as long as she could sleep under the stars and moon. The cowboy smiled and said there was no better place.

Later that night, as they bedded down on separate bedrolls with the fire between them, Spur was remembering all the nights he'd spent sleeping out just like this one. Most of the time, he slept alone, but tonight he was sharing it with a lady who had deep blue eyes. Watching her from across the fire as she slept, he longed to understand the attraction that had come over him. It was a feeling that wasn't making any sense to the old cowboy. Was it love? No, it couldn't be love. He had only loved one woman in all his years, and she was gone. Was it lust? Nah, it wasn't lusting. Those days were few and far between. And then it hit him. It was a revelation that could only come as he lay under the starry sky listening to the music of the coyotes. In the stillness, the wind whispered he was not in love with this hippy chick; he was in love with the life she lived. She represented everything that he loved in this life. She had a cowboy's heart.

Of course! That's what attracted Spur. The one thing that he loved the most was the one thing that was slipping away. There were more paved roads and towns filling up with folks that no longer showed respect for others. Also, folks no longer wandered down an unknown path just to see where it led. Opinions today were more and more just arguments, and they weren't honest about what they think. He was finding it harder and harder to just layout under a star-filled sky and enjoy the beautiful night music. This hippy chick was living life as he had always lived life.

That night Spur did something he had not done since he was abandoned so many years ago on the streets of Boston—he cried.

Acknowledgements

How do I adequately thank everyone who has contributed to this latest collection of tales? For me, it begins with acknowledging the unmeasurable contribution of my good friend, Paul Juhasz. Paul, your insight into the underlying meaning behind many of these tales blew me away, and your suggestions, along with your editing, made these stories work. Again my friend, thank you for keeping me writing even when I didn't want to. Also, thanks for letting me borrow your creation—the character of Big Tuna. I return him hopefully unscathed.

I will always have a deep appreciation and love for the friendship and support of Julie Chappell and Hank Jones. You both believed in me enough to encourage me to keep writing. And thanks, Hank, for the boat ride with Paul on Lake Keystone that began "Paid in Full." So glad it was only fiction.

I am fortunate to have friends who also believed in my crazy tales enough to keep them in the public eye. Mallory Young, you never failed to subject your students to these stories, and you did it with such enthusiasm that I began to believe the tales had some value.

My good friend, David Price (the character of Tom in "The Glass Factory Menagerie,") I can't thank you enough for sharing the first book with so many of your friends. Hope this collection is worthy of your patronage of love.

Next up are the guys that I call the original Violated Onions (Mike, Jessie, Tim, Rick, Ronnie, and of course, Hank). Thanks for laughing at my exaggerated and often unbelievable stories. I lift my glass to you, gentlemen.

Again I cannot say enough about how grateful I am for the support and professionalism of Fine Dog Press and Roxie and Terry Kirk. Let's make more books!

Finally, I want to always remember and thank my lovely lady, Kelli who has stood by my side and all the creative craziness that I cycled through. You made my wandering cease. I love you, Bud.

About the Author

Woodstok Farley is a wanderer. He wandered far from his south Florida home to the great southwest. He finally settled on his bride's land, and they began to raise a son along with a menagerie of animals and mesquite trees. His first collection of short stories entitled *As the Wave Rose: Florida Tales and Other Wandering Stories,* published by Fine Dog Press, displays his deep yearning to return to the seacoast. Woodstok's second collection, *The Water Stop Saloon: More Wandering Tales,* finds him now yearning for answers to the questions his travels have brought him.

www.ingramcontent.com/pod-product-compliance
Ingram Content Group UK Ltd.
Pitfield, Milton Keynes, MK11 3LW, UK
UKHW041301180426
11947UKWH00009B/604